# *Meet the Deadliest Rescue Force in the World*

MARK STONE. He's a man with a mission. A former Green Beret and ex-P.O.W. who's devoted his life to finding America's forgotten soldiers in Vietnam and freeing them from their hell on Earth. His rescue tactics are unique—and quite lethal.

HOG WILEY. He's a good ole boy from East Texas—and one of the deadliest mercenaries money can buy. This burly bulk of southern-fried fury loves fighting almost as much as he loves whiskey and women. And that's why he's perfect for Stone's team.

TERRANCE LOUGHLIN. He's a steely British commando with a refined taste for culture—and total destruction. Explosives are his specialty, but this tough Englishman can fill a walking target with bullets like a master assassin.

*These guys are the very best. And the U.S. government knows it. In fact, they may be America's only hope in the most desperate international situations.*

*No job is too tough for. . .*

# *Stone: M.I.A. Hunter*

Don't Miss the Others in This Action-Packed Series!

Y0-AGQ-163

# STONE

# M.I.A. HUNTER

## INVASION U.S.S.R.

### JACK BUCHANAN

JOVE BOOKS, NEW YORK

STONE: M.I.A. HUNTER
INVASION U.S.S.R.

A Jove Book/published by arrangement with
the author

PRINTING HISTORY
Jove edition/April 1988

ISBN: 0-515-09564-8

Jove Books are published by The Berkley Publishing Group,
200 Madison Avenue, New York, New York 10016.
The name "JOVE" and the "J" logo
are trademarks belonging to Jove Publications, Inc.

PRINTED IN THE UNITED STATES OF AMERICA

10  9  8  7  6  5  4  3  2  1

*"Go with us as we seek to defend the defense-less and to free the enslaved."*

—from the "Special Forces Prayer"

# Chapter One

It was an hour after midnight. Lee Daniels moved between several desks in the long office, his tiny penlight flicking across polished surfaces. The file cabinet he sought was there, in the corner.

Was that a noise in the corridor outside?

He stood perfectly still in the darkness. The room smelled of oil and something bitter, and it was cold. There was no sound. He took a long breath. He moved again, shuffling between chairs and desks with just a touch of light, on then off. He reached out to touch the cabinet. Then paused again, listening. *Was* that a sound? Or was he just nervous as hell?

Whatever it was, it wasn't repeated. He took out the pointed steel tool that he would have to use to break the lock. Inserting one end into the crack of the cabinet door, he began to lever it. He gritted his teeth, muscling it—and the door gave with a loud *snap*.

He glanced around the dim room cautiously. He be-

lieved for some time he was under suspicion by the
K.G.B. How many times had he noticed that he was
being followed? Surely *that* was not paranoia. Of
course, the K.G.B. might take it into its head to suspect
any one of a thousand foreigners in Moscow. . .

But under suspicion or not, this new angle had to be
investigated. He gently pulled open the cabinet door; it
slid on silky rollers. He had paid dearly for the information that had located this particular cabinet. Gennadi had
sworn he'd seen the file only that morning. Could Gennadi be trusted? Daniels shook his head. Maybe, and
maybe not. But he had to follow through.

His fingers flicked through the folders as he held the
tiny flash with his mouth. The folder should be labeled:
Class D Monitors. Gennadi had even written it out for
him.

There was no folder with that label.

Daniels swore and went back through them again.
No—no folder with that label. Damn.

The noise again. He switched off the light and silently pushed the drawer closed. It sounded like a cough
from the corridor.

He had been here long enough. He couldn't search
the entire room.

He had better execute that old army routine—get the
hell out while he was still in one large piece. He pocketed the tool and moved toward the end of the room.

And immediately a light went on at the opposite end.

Daniels dropped to hands and knees thinking this was
a hell of an attitude for a respected journalist, crawling
along an office floor in a highly secret installation in the
middle of Moscow.

There was a door in front of him. He could see the
knob and the glass panel. Someone was speaking in a

low voice behind him, probably fifty feet away. Another voice answered. Maybe he had tripped a silent alarm, and they had come to investigate.

He reached the door and felt for the knob. It was not locked. He turned the knob and opened the door far enough to crawl through. Closing the door carefully, he peered around. He was in another office, this one lined with books. It had two tables and a row of chairs and there was another door, standing open, on the far side.

He crawled across the room to the open door and stood up cautiously. And as he did so someone played a powerful flashlight on the room—and caught him full in the middle of it!

There was a shout and Daniels heard running feet. He slammed the door, felt for the lock, and clicked it. Dashing across another room, he opened a door and came out in a dark corridor.

He had a vague plan of the building in his mind. He turned right, toward what he thought would be the back of the building.

And a bell began clanging.

He ran to the end of the corridor and bounded down the cement steps to the fourth floor.

This corridor was carpeted. He ran toward the front of the building, hoping to throw off pursuit. He could hear voices: men were shouting orders; it sounded like a dozen of them.

He stopped suddenly. It sounded as if men were coming up the stairs in front of him. Instantly he tried the first knob. The door was locked. He tried the next and it turned. He slid inside the room, easing the door shut. Leaning against the door, he got his breath back. Men ran past outside.

Opening the door, he peeked out. The corridor was

empty. He ran toward the front again and down the stairs. The corridor was different from the others. It was very narrow and did not run all the way to the front windows. He could hear echoing voices. It was hard to tell where they came from. He opened a door and slid inside.

He was in a laboratory.

It was dark and shadowy but there was reflected light from the outside, enough to see by. He moved to the windows. They were thick glass bound with metal and opened by turning a crank. He cranked one open and looked out and down. There was a yard below, with half a dozen trucks standing silent by a tall fence.

Many buildings in Russia had rope fire escapes; he had seen them many times. He looked for one now. There were no ordinary escapes outside the windows. He was in luck. He found one coiled up behind some boxes under the next window. Quickly he tossed the coil out the window and tied the end to the crank. In another moment he climbed through the window, grasped the rope, and began to let himself down.

It was a four-foot drop to the hard ground and he ran for one of the trucks, an old Chevrolet. He could see the gate was locked but it did not look impregnable. As he flung the car door open he heard a shout. Someone had spotted him.

A shot followed. The bullet spanged off the side of the truck. Daniels jumped inside and turned the switch. The starter ground for a moment, then the engine caught and blossomed into a roar. Another shot hit the side, then two more. He put the truck in gear. A shot shattered the side-view mirror.

He gave it the gas and, hunched over, steered for the gate.

A machine pistol stuttered somewhere behind him and bullets spattered the rear end of the truck just as he hit the gate, smashing it like kindling. Pieces flew; one big chunk dropped on the hood and slithered off as he made a fast turn into a dark street.

The shooting stopped abruptly. He was out of range.

The truck smelled abominably inside the cab. Daniels looked automatically at the gas gauge. Half full. He was on a narrow street lined by dark buildings. At the first intersection he turned right, then turned left again on a large, wider street. The speedometer said he was doing about forty. There was almost no traffic.

Where the hell was he going?

He ought to dump the truck as soon as he could and get onto the Metro. He began to look for Metro stops. It was an old truck that rattled and squeaked. In the U.S. it would have been junked long since.

Now was the time he needed the C.I.A.! They were sweet enough when they wanted something from him, but were the occasional news tips they fed him good enough for this?

He passed Leningrad Prospekt. Damn. He should have turned. The Metro ran along there. He tried to look behind him. If he swerved the truck a little he could get a look. There were lights back there. A car was following.

He slowed the truck and turned off into a small shadowy street, then gave it the gas. In a moment he saw the flash of car lights. They were following, all right. And they probably had twice the speed of this old clunker.

He turned into an alley.

The old truck coughed and slowed suddenly. He pumped the gas pedal and the Chevy gasped and took heart for half a block, then coughed again and stopped.

Daniels piled out and ran. The truck was blocking the alley; the car could not get past. Could he outrun them? He was thirty-four now and not the college athlete he had once been. If he could get back to the Metro . . .

A car turned into the alley ahead of him.

So they were in radio communication. He turned right and went over a fence.

He was in a small garden with strings and wire netting and it was pitch dark. In a moment he was hopelessly tangled. He stopped struggling and lay still. Maybe they hadn't seen where he'd gone.

But they had. A powerful flashlight spotted him, and burly men came over the fence and hauled him out of the garden.

None of them spoke English. Or none admitted it. They took him back to one of the cars and pushed him in. Two men got in beside him and another drove, backing the car out of the alley.


Daniels was taken to the K.G.B. building at Dzerzhinsky Square. He had been here often as a newsman, but this time they led him through a small door into a long corridor, into an elevator, and up to an unfamiliar part of the building.

He was put into a small, cold room and left. There was a large window to the corridor and a guard outside the door. He sat down to wait.

He had had the presence of mind to drop the steel lever he'd used on the cabinet, so he had nothing incriminating on his person.

Two hours dragged by. Now and then he got up and paced the tiny room, then sat again. There was nothing to read, nothing to see but the guard's broad back.

Another hour went by.

A man came in quickly, a thin, intense-looking man with black brows and hollow cheeks. He was dressed in a dark blue suit and looked, Daniels thought, like an insurance salesman.

He introduced himself. "I am Colonel Zarnov."

Daniels got up. "You will take me to the American Embassy?"

Zarnov almost smiled. His English was quite good. "I do not believe you understand your situation, Mr. Daniels."

"I am an American citizen."

Zarnov shrugged. "You are a spy. That is all that concerns us at the moment."

"Whatever you charge me with, I demand to see the American authorities."

"That is out of the question."

"Are you arresting me?"

Zarnov nodded. "But there will be no notification to the American Embassy."

"Why not?"

"My dear Mr. Daniels. This is the Soviet Union. Our rules are not the same as yours. Are you prepared to tell us everything you have already passed on to the C.I.A.? I will have a stenographer brought in."

"You can't do this."

Zarnov's brows raised. "I am afraid we can. We are the K.G.B., Mr. Daniels. We can do anything we wish."

"There is such a thing as international law!"

"I have heard of it."

Daniels controlled his temper. "At least give me your assurance that you will inform my embassy that I have been arrested."

"That would not be strictly true."

"What?"

"You are interested in truth, are you not, Mr. Daniels? So I will be very truthful with you. In this matter you have been more than arrested."

"More than—? How do you mean?"

"I mean, you have disappeared."

# Chapter Two

Mark Stone stood in the deep shadow of a group of pines and looked at the luminous dial of his watch. He was a big man, dressed in camouflage fatigues. His reflexes were those of a hunting panther. He was armed with two of his favorite weapons: an Uzi machine pistol, and a .44 magnum in a soft leather holster under his arm.

It was very dark. He touched Hog Wiley and pointed to the left. Hog was a huge, powerful fighting machine from Texas, often rude and uncouth, but no one was as good in a tight place. Hog nodded and moved away. They were moving in on three posted sentries.

Stone looked at Terrance Loughlin and pointed right. Loughlin nodded and moved silently. He was a former Commando of the British Special Air Service.

Stone moved forward. They had done this many times before and each man knew precisely what the other would do.

Stone went to his knees and lay flat, contemplating the terrain just ahead of him. He could see the sentries. They were in a hastily dug trench and they had not yet camouflaged the parapet of fresh dirt. He shook his head. Careless. Did they think themselves safe because they were in a trench?

He slithered forward, counting.

When he got to fifty he was at the parapet, lying full length in the tall grass. Any second now he would hear Wiley's attack.

It came in another second, a distinct *bonk*.

The sentry in front of him rose an inch and turned his head. Stone was over the parapet in an instant, the .44 magnum in the man's face. "Don't move a muscle."

He saw a scared, white face. The sentry nodded, licking his lips. "W—where'd you come from?"

A sergeant walked out of the night. He waved his arm to someone behind him. "All right. Turn on the lights."

Immediately several floodlights illuminated the scene.

Wiley had brought his fist down atop a sentry's helmet, flooring the man. Loughlin had a bayonet at a sentry's throat.

The sergeant motioned the three men to gather in front of him. "All three of you are dead."

One said, "But we were watching—"

"You thought you were watching, but you saw *nothing*." He indicated Stone and the others. "Now you know what you're up against. If this had been the real thing, I repeat, you'd all be dead."

Stone said, "You have to know what to watch for."

"That's right," the sergeant agreed. "Let's move to the next position and try it again."

"Jesus!" one of the trainees said. "It's impossible for guys to do what you just did!"

Loughlin laughed. "Let me tell you a secret, lad."

"What?"

"All you do is make yourself invisible."

The trainees sighed. The sergeant snapped his fingers. "All right, you guys, shake a leg."

Loughlin said quietly, "Jeep coming."

Stone turned his head, listening. He glanced at the sergeant and the trainees. None of them heard the vehicle for another thirty seconds.

There was a weedy, two-track road that led to the training grounds from the main road. The jeep came out of the shadows, running with slit lights, and pulled up behind them.

Carol Jenner sat behind the steering wheel.

"Hey!" Hog yelled, "Look who's here!"

"Where did you drop from, precious?" Loughlin asked with pleasure.

"I came to corral you guys, of course. You're wanted at headquarters."

Stone shrugged. "Well, sorry, Sergeant. When you gotta go, you gotta go."

"You guys must really rate," the sergeant grunted. "Pretty girls never come out here in the field after me."

Loughlin got into the jeep. "Some of us got it, Sergeant. Some of us don't."

The sergeant sighed, watching them pile in. The jeep made a circle and headed away. He said aloud, "Yeah, and some of us just get the clap."

The jeep bumped over the rutted road and came out onto the pavement, heading for the HQ buildings of Fort Bragg. Hog asked, "What they got for us, honey?"

"I don't know a thing," Carol said. "All I can tell you is, your vacation is over."

"I bet we're going to Africa," Hog grunted. "Straighten out that feller in Libya. What's his name? Kadaffy?"

"Naw." Loughlin shook his head. "We're slated to stop that war in the Middle East."

"Or the Philippines," Stone chuckled.

"Okay, which is it, honey?" Hog asked.

Carol shook her head, grinning around at them. "I have no idea."

"You know how curious we are," Hog urged. "Guess a little."

She laughed and gave him a look. "Orders is orders, Tex." She speeded up. "Besides, you'll know soon enough."

Carol drove them to a long, low building, stopped to show a pass to an alert sentry who looked at all of them and then nodded. She let them out at a door. "They're waiting for you inside."

A corporal was seated at a small desk just inside the door. He jumped up as they entered.

"This way, please." He led them down the corridor and opened a door. They filed inside and the door closed. It was a small room with no windows. It contained five chairs, a table, and a bench against one wall. There were blackboards on two walls and a clock.

Senator Jerome Harler got up from a chair and came toward them, hand outstretched. "Well, we meet again! Good to see you, Mark, Terrance, Hog."

"This is a surprise, Senator," Stone said. Harler was the man responsible for initiating the presidential pardon clearing the three of them for "crimes" committed in the course of their unsanctioned search-and-rescue missions for American servicemen still held in Southeast Asia. Harler had believed in them when others in the government had condemned them, and Harler had won out.

Hog grinned. "Anybody you want taken care of, Senator?"

Harler grinned back. "There are a few in the Senate I'd like to turn you loose on . . ."

"Just say the word," Loughlin told him.

Harler was a thin, sallow man with glasses. He looked as if he had been feeding the pigs and forking hay all day and had just put on his best clothes. His hayseed appearance concealed one of the best minds in Congress.

He indicated the chairs. "Sit down. Let me tell you a story." He thrust hands in his pockets. "I know it's only been three weeks since your last mission and I don't know if you're getting restless or rusty."

"You want us to go back to Asia?" Hog asked.

Harler shook his head. "There's been no new intelligence on living M.I.A./P.O.W.'s there for you to work on, unfortunately. But something else has come up." He smiled at them. "When we pull you out in the middle of the night I'm sure you suspect we think it's important."

Harler paused. No one said a thing. He continued: "I have a ticking time bomb of a mission for you, men. I am heading a fact-finding committee overseas. We leave within hours. I want you to come along with me."

"Where to, Senator?"

"Moscow."

"Uh-*huh*," Loughlin grunted.

"I've been planning this trip for some time," Harler said, "but something has cropped up that will take your expertise. It'll be a good way to get you into the country. You'll be part of my security staff."

"What cropped up?" Stone asked.

"A journalist named Lee Daniels has disappeared. We want him found. He worked for the C.I.A. I've requested you be assigned to this because Daniels is missing in action, even though unofficially."

"Disappeared inside Russia?"

"In Moscow to be exact. He is undoubtedly being held by the K.G.B. and being interrogated."

Stone said, "He knows things he shouldn't tell?"

"Precisely. He also knows things he should tell us. And aside from all that, we don't like it one damn bit that the K.G.B. thinks it can grab an American citizen off the Russian street any damn time it wants to and hold him prisoner."

"Surely the State Department is protesting."

"The Soviet government officially claims to have no knowledge of Daniels's whereabouts. They insist they are doing everything possible to locate him." Harler made a face. "That is all good-quality bullshit. We know they have him."

"Isn't the C.I.A. in on this?"

Harler nodded. "Up to their ears." He smiled at them. "But I know damn well the C.I.A. doesn't have anyone with your qualifications. I'm counting on you to dig into this, and get Daniels out of Russia by hook or by crook. I don't care how you do it and I don't care whose ass you kick." He took a breath. "I didn't say any of that."

Stone smiled. "We understand."

"It'll take time for them to break Daniels down. He's a good, husky young man. I suppose they'll use drugs on him. There may still be time to get to him."

Stone asked, "And when they get what they want from him?"

Harler said bluntly, "Then they'll kill him. They'll take the body out to the middle of Siberia and bury it deeper than hell and shower us with reports on how they're looking everywhere for him."

"Not really good," Loughlin said moodily.

"They can't torture him, then let him go. He's a journalist and he'd write what happened to him. Even if the bleeding hearts defend the K.G.B., a hell of a lot of people will believe Daniels. So he'll remain 'missing' until the end of time."

Hog said, "He could be dead already, Senator."

"Yes, I know that. But we've got to try."

# Chapter Three

Daniels was taken downstairs at Colonel Zarnov's orders, put into a closed van, and driven away. It was cold, the van leaked air, and there was nothing to hold on to. The driver took corners like a maniac. Daniels cursed him all the way.

They finally slowed and entered a building; he could tell from the sound. When the van stopped, the doors were opened and three uniformed men stared at him. One said in good English, "Get out."

He climbed out feeling bruised, and they took his arms and walked him inside to a hallway. Daniels asked the English-speaking guard, "Where are we?"

"No talking," the man said.

They pushed him into a small, brightly lighted room and slammed the door.

Another long wait. The room had no windows and only two metal chairs, both bolted to the floor. There was nothing else in the room. The light fixture was encased in a metal mesh affair that looked as if it would withstand a cannon shell. It was on the ceiling in the exact center of the white-painted room.

After a couple hours, a man in a white jacket opened the door and beckoned him. "Come with me, please."

Daniels stood. "What is this place?"

In heavily accented English the man repeated, "Come with me, please."

He looked like a wrestler, Daniels thought. Sighing inwardly, he obeyed. The man led him down a hall and into an elevator. They went up four floors and got off. The corridor was dark gray with a yellow stripe down the middle. On either side were doors, each with a small square window. Daniels had the feeling it was a prison.

"What is this place?" he asked again.

The man did not answer. They walked down the hall nearly to the end. Producing a ring of keys, the man opened a door and motioned him in.

Daniels glanced down the hallway and the man said, "Do not try it."

"If you're going to keep me here, what does it matter if you tell me where I am?"

"I obey my orders. Please go in."

Daniels looked into the cell, hesitating.

The man said, "I will have to put you in."

"All right." Daniels went in and the door closed behind him. He was in a small square cell, probably three paces in each direction. There was a cot fastened to the wall, a toilet and basin, and several metal pegs high on the wall. A tiny square window showed a bit of sky— and nothing else.

"Home sweet home," Daniels muttered. "Shit."

• • •

A great many things had to be done at once. Hog Wiley spent an hour and a half in a barber chair getting his beard trimmed, his hair cut, and his nails looked after. Stone and Loughlin were not emergency cases.

However, it was necessary for all three to dress properly as members of a United States senator's entourage. None of them owned a suit. Several tailors were put to work altering and sewing, and when they dressed in front of mirrors, the change was incredible. Wiley was most uncomfortable, feeling decidedly out of place and somewhat out of sorts.

"I look like a goddamn used-car salesman!"

Stone reassured him, "You look fine, Hog. Like a wrestler on his day off."

Hog looked very suspicious. "Is that a compliment?"

The senator was able to get forged documents and passes finished in a remarkably short time. Passport pictures were taken and processed, connection passes made, and Customs experts went over every article of clothing and equipment, making certain everything would pass muster by the Customs people of the U.S.S.R.

Their weapons had to be left behind.

Senator Harler said, "Our agents inside the Soviet Union will find you arms and whatever else you need."

And when all was ready, they rushed off to the airport.

The flight to Moscow was an anticlimax. With everything completed, the team slept most of the way.

An hour before landing, Harler had a quiet talk with Stone.

"Your C.I.A. contact in Moscow will be Jim Leech. He's a veteran and knows Russia." He opened an envelope and took out a snapshot. "This is Leech, taken less than two months ago."

Stone looked at a man of about forty, a square no-nonsense face with deep creases.

Harler said, "I'll get hold of him when we arrive and he will contact you. He'll know best how to do that." At Stone's look he smiled. "The Russkis have bugs everywhere. You may find one in your soup. They're the most suspicious people in the world. Never say anything important on the telephone and don't talk in your rooms."

"Who was it who said: 'Silence is never your enemy'?"

Harler nodded. "Remember that in the Soviet Union."

"How do you do business?"

"Very damn carefully." Harler lit a cigarette. "I am sure the Russians—I mean the K.G.B. of course—are going to be very suspicious of you and your team very quickly. Because in order to carry out your mission you're going to have to be away much of the time, and not with me as you're supposed to be. They will pick up on that."

"Well, we're used to tight spots, Senator."

"Not like in Russia. Take nothing at face value and be cautious about everything. The K.G.B. is capable of anything."

He left Stone some maps of Moscow, which he studied with Wiley and Loughlin till the plane lowered the flaps for landing.

# Chapter Four

Russian Customs routinely searched all the luggage and found nothing. Stone thought they looked hard at him, Hog, and Loughlin, three big tough-looking men, but no one was pulled out of line.

An embassy staff man had two cars waiting for them and they piled in with luggage and were whisked away to the embassy on the Garden Ring.

The cars halted in a courtyard and a uniformed marine led them inside to a warm sitting room. "There's a coffee shop just down the corridor," he told them. "Mr. Davison will be here to see you in a moment or two."

"Thanks," Stone said.

Davison showed up promptly. He was a skinny, smiling man with horn-rimmed glasses. "I'll show you to your quarters, gentlemen."

"Are we to stay here in the embassy?"

Davison shrugged. "You're supposed to be Senator Harler's security people. We have listed you as such."

Stone nodded. "It would look wrong for us to stay outside the embassy."

"We think so." Davison indicated their luggage. "If you will bring that, we'll go along to the other wing."

As they passed a small waiting room, Davison halted. A woman and a small boy were seated inside. Davison said, "Daniels's wife and son. Let's say a word to them."

"Tell the kid to eat his grits," Hog commented.

Giving him a look, Stone entered the room and went to the woman. She was a brunette, not a beauty but not plain either. She had obviously been crying but she was doing her best to bear up. Davison introduced the three of them. "These men are going to help find your husband, Mrs. Daniels."

She had noticed them, now she looked at them again. She nodded and sighed, and tried a small smile. "Russia is a big place. Isn't it an impossible job?"

"Don't be pessimistic," Davison told her.

"If the Russians don't want him found . . ." She shook her head. "I'm sorry we ever came to this miserable city."

"The government is putting pressure on the Kremlin," Davison assured her. "And these men have a remarkable record in finding people who have been hidden away."

"The impossible only takes a little longer," Hog said. "Don't give up."

She smiled at him and looked a little brighter when they left, Stone thought.

Three rooms had been assigned to them. Each was only a cubicle, not even as large as an average cheap motel room in Kansas, but comfortable. Each had a single bed, chest of drawers, mirror, one chair, and a lighting fixture; a tiny bathroom containing a stall shower, and an area rug on the floor.

"Home, sweet home," Loughlin said.

"Well, they're spartan rooms," Davison admitted. "But they tell me you people could sleep on a buzz saw and not notice it."

"Hell, we do that all the time," Hog grunted.

Stone asked, "How about our comings and goings? I mean, how do we get in and out of the embassy?"

Davison nodded. "You don't want to be seen using the front entrance."

"Right."

"Well, we have several entrances. I'll show them to you when you're ready." He gave each of them a card and a small folder. "The card has my telephone number and the folder shows the plan of the embassy, especially two floors." He put his finger on Stone's folder. "Your rooms are here. The cafeteria is here—and so on. They're marked. You all have ID. Show it on demand and if you have any problems at all, call me, day or night. Okay?"

"Good."

"Any questions?"

Stone asked, "What about Jim Leech?"

"He's C.I.A. Out of my department." Davison shrugged. "He'll contact you himself. He's been told you're here. Anything else?"

"How 'bout some chow?" Hog suggested. "I could eat a cow my own self."

The call from agent Jim Leech came late that evening. Stone took it in Davison's office on the scrambler.

Leech asked, "Settled in?"

"Yes."

"Good. I can't come to the embassy. Meet me at the Kiev Station Square. Look on a map. I'll be in the garden with a rolled-up newspaper."

He hung up and Stone asked Davison, "Why doesn't he come here?"

"I have no idea."

"Does the K.G.B. know who he is?"

"I'm certain they do."

"Where's the Kiev Station?"

Davison showed him on a large map. It was close by, within easy walking distance.

In his room he told the others about the call. Hog made a face. "Let's slide up on it from three sides."

Loughlin cocked an eye at him. "You don't trust the C.I.A.?"

"Ain't this Russia? Pardon me while I check m'own fingerprints."

Pulling on a coat, Loughlin said, "I feel damn naked without a weapon."

"I assume that's part of what we're seeing Leech about. Let's get moving."

The air outside was crisp, not the bitter cold of winter, but not spring either. It had rained lightly that day but there was no ice on the streets.

It was not a long walk to the Kiev Station. Pedestrians were few, most hurrying along as if late for something; few cars were about, though a dozen heavily laden trucks passed by. They crossed the Moskva River on the Kutuzov Bridge, then walked along the river, separating before they got close.

Stone would go straight in with Hog and Loughlin circling around, keeping him in sight.

Stone turned right as he approached the station and walked into the square. There were trees and benches, grassy plots where tots doubtless played during the day, and a large round pond. No one sat on the benches and only a few people strode rapidly through the square.

Then a man detached himself from a smaller building and walked to intercept Stone. He carried a rolled-up newspaper, which he slapped against his leg, as if to call attention to it.

Stone slowed his pace, watching the other. He was a stocky, dark-haired man wearing the familiar fur head-piece many Russians preferred. His long overcoat was unbuttoned, one hand in a pocket. He had seen Stone and turned toward him as if expectant.

But he was not the man in the photograph Senator Harler had shown Stone on the plane. This was not Jim Leech!

Stone halted suddenly. This would alert Hog and Loughlin.

Then he turned about and began walking away. He heard his name called and looked over his shoulder as the man pulled a long-barreled pistol from the pocket and extended his arm.

In the next second he stiffened and went to his knees, dropping the gun.

Stone ran back as Hog and Loughlin converged. The man with the newspaper was dead, a knife buried in his side. It was Hog's knife, Stone saw instantly. In the gloom he hadn't even seen Hog throw it.

Hog reached the body first and pulled the blade out, wiping it on the downed man's overcoat. Stone said, "Thanks." He slipped the silenced pistol into his coat.

Loughlin frisked the body, turning up another pistol, which he pocketed. Then he dragged the body off the path into a fringe of shrubs. They walked on as if nothing had happened. It had all taken only a moment.

"Who was he?" Hog asked.

"Maybe K.G.B.," Stone said. "He knew where we were to meet. I wonder if they got Leech. I wonder if it was even Leech on the phone."

They moved out of the square and strode down a street of apartments.

Loughlin said, "So he knew we were unarmed and figured to get all of us, one after the other."

"Pretty damn sure of himself," Hog commented.

"Now what?" asked Loughlin. "Do we go back to the embassy?"

Stone motioned. "Duck in here. There's a truck following us." There was an open space between two large apartment houses. Stone glanced back. The truck was coming without lights, a very suspicious circumstance.

They passed an area of children's swings and slides and hurried along under trees, toward an open area. The truck had halted and men were spilling out.

The man in the overcoat had had accomplices. Maybe they had arrived a moment too late at the square.

"This way," Hog hissed at them. He turned abruptly and ran close to the buildings, ducking under an arbor. They came to a line of smaller buildings and halted in deep shadow, looking back. The men from the truck were spreading out around the open area at the command of an officer.

"Too many of them," Loughlin said softly.

Stone pointed to a low fence and Hog went over it in one smooth leap. Loughlin followed and a dog began to bark to their right. It was a small, yappy dog in an open window and Stone cursed him. The officer behind them shouted and a squad of men turned their way.

Diving over the fence, Stone ran after Loughlin. Hog had found a ramp and had run down it, opened a door into a building, and disappeared inside. A shot spattered the stucco over his head and Stone ducked, sprinting down the ramp. Loughlin held the door open for him and a fusillade of shots smashed the building where he had been a second before.

"This way," Hog yelled. He was in a corridor, shiny with tile. They clattered after him, made a turn, and found a stairway.

The pursuers were at the door. It clanged open.

Hog, at the top of the steps, had a door open. "Shake your ass—"

Loughlin slammed the door as Stone went through. He fiddled with the lock, swearing softly. It clicked and he ran after Stone.

They were in a hallway with a dozen or more doors on each side. A woman looked out at them, then closed the door quickly. Stone followed Hog to the front of the building. The big Texan opened a door cautiously, peering out to the street.

"The truck is up there, facing the other way. I don't see anybody—"

Stone reached up and unscrewed a light bulb. "Let's get across the street. They may radio for help."

Hog led the way again. No one yelled as they crossed the open area. In the shadow of the building, he paused. "We're gonna have to hole up somewhere, ain't we?"

Loughlin said, "I hear apartments are hard to get in this town."

"We could get on a waiting list maybe," Hog agreed.

"Get moving," Stone said. "Let's get the hell out of this area."

Hog started out, then stopped. He looked back at Stone and pointed. A jeeplike car turned into the street. In it were four men, one with a powerful light that he began to play on the buildings on the opposite side of the street.

"Inside," Stone said. "In the first door—quick!"

They very nearly made it. But the light caught one of them and there was a shout. Stone slammed the door, found a bolt, and pushed it shut. A round smashed the panel an inch above his head as he turned to run.

A half dozen shots ripped through the door. Stone threw himself flat, yelling, "Down!"

He saw Hog and Loughlin hit the deck as the lead screamed overhead and chewed up the wall. Instantly they were all up and running. The corridor ran straight back to the rear door. Halfway there Stone heard them pounding the front door, then shooting the lock off.

Turning, he fired the silenced pistol, one, two, three, four shots. The sounds at the door stopped abruptly, then he heard a wail.

Loughlin yelled, "Come on, come on—"

They ran out into an alley and turned left. *What the hell had happened to Jim Leech?*

Loughlin was in the lead. He halted abruptly and pointed to the right. Stone saw a van parked there in an alcove. It was some dark color and might have been a Moskvich.

"Can you drive it?"

Loughlin nodded. "I can drive anything with wheels."

The van was locked but it took Hog only a moment to pry the door open and slide inside. Loughlin got behind the wheel and fiddled with wires, muttering to himself. In a moment he chuckled. "Got it!" The engine turned over, protesting, blowing out clouds of smoke. "She's a clunker," he said.

"Let's get outa here," Hog urged.

Loughlin backed the van out into the alley and the gears ground; the car slowly took heart as he pumped petrol to it. "Come on, baby . . . move your ass . . ."

Stone said, "Lights behind us. Move this thing!"

Loughlin coaxed the van down the alley, gaining speed with the headlights off. He put his head out the window for better vision.

Stone looked back. The car behind them wasn't gaining—maybe hadn't seen them in the dark. Someone was using a powerful spotlight, shining it into every suspicious corner.

Loughlin grinned at them. "I think we made it, mates."

They came to an intersection, turned right.

And there, a jeep was halted—with two militiamen pointing rifles at them.

# Chapter Five

"Oh *shit!*" Loughlin said. He hunched over the wheel. "Hang on everybody!" He put the pedal to the floor.

Stone heard a yell. He snapped a shot at the men in the jeep. The old van hit the other car, a glancing blow, metal screaming. The jeep turned over gracefully, in slow motion. A submachine gun fired into the sky. Then they were past, thundering down a wide boulevard.

Hog yelled, "Get our asses the hell off this street!"

Loughlin turned the van at the first cross street and took the turn on two wheels. There was a heavy *klunk!* as the van settled back on all four wheels; it seemed to groan and fishtailed for a moment as Loughlin fought the steering wheel.

Then he grinned at them again. "Made it, chums. Anybody hurt?"

"Jesus!" Hog said admiringly. "They could use you at Indianapolis! You been eatin' grits again?"

Stone said, "Nobody behind us. Watch your speed."

Loughlin let up on the gas and the old van chugged along more sedately. "Where to?"

"Find a public telephone," Stone said. "We'll call the embassy."

"Are public phones bugged?"

"Even if they are, we've got to chance it. Where can we find a pay phone?" Stone scratched his chin.

"In a bus station?" Hog suggested.

"Good idea," Stone agreed. "Find a bus station."

Near Gorky Park Loughlin noticed a Metro station. "Try that. I'll park this clunker and wait."

"Right." Stone jumped out of the van as Loughlin killed the engine. He walked into the station and saw a bank of telephones near a news kiosk. Inserting two kopecks, he dialed the embassy and asked for Davison.

"Just a moment, sir."

It took a minute for Davison to come on the line. He sounded as if he'd just been awakened. "Davison."

Stone spoke rapidly. "Leech didn't show. The bad guys jumped us."

Davison didn't hesitate. "Don't give me the answer. You know how to walk from home to first?"

"Yes."

"Meet me that many miles north of here." He hung up.

Stone went back to the van and squeezed in. "We'll meet Davison four miles north of the embassy. Let's go."

"How'd you figure that out without telling the K.G.B.?" Loughlin asked.

"We're hoping the K.G.B. doesn't know baseball."

"Oh. Right-o." Loughlin put the van in gear and swung around to head back.

Stone asked, "What's in the back of this thing?"

"Nuttin'," Hog said. "The van's empty. Will they follow Davison?"

"Not unless they surround the embassy. He'll be out before they can do it."

"God willing," Loughlin said.

The old van had a gas gauge and an odometer. Hog checked the miles as they passed the embassy, calling out half miles as they approached four.

Davison was on a bicycle. They came up beside him and stopped. Hog jumped out, opened the rear door of the van, put the bike in, and climbed in himself. Davison took his seat in front.

"So you guys are in trouble already?"

Stone explained what had happened at the Kiev Station. Davison shook his head and sighed. "The clandestine war goes on. You killed this guy?"

"Very dead," Loughlin said.

Stone asked, "Have you heard from Jim Leech?"

"Nothing. *I* haven't heard. But that doesn't mean someone in the embassy hasn't. C.I.A. is not my chunk. I'll make inquiries."

Stone said, "Do we assume the K.G.B. knows about us—will they know names and descriptions?"

"You were probably photographed when you went through Customs. They have the data from your passports. By now I'm sure they know a lot about you. And since what happened at the Kiev Station, they'll want to haul you in."

"They tried," Loughlin said cheerfully.

Davison said, "We'll get you new passports—different names and such. It may help. I brought along some money." He handed it over. "And some info. This is the address of a safe house." He gave Stone a small card.

"We keep a number of rooms here and there just in case."

"There's a name here," Stone said, reading the card.

"Yes. Rima Suslov. She's one of ours. You go to that address tonight and she'll show up in the morning. She's a good, tough gal, brought up in Moscow and Denver, Colorado. Suslov is not her real name. Her parents were murdered by Stalin because they were Jewish. She'll interpret for you and give you advice. She's employed by *Tass* as a translator."

"Good show," Loughlin said.

"Where did you get this van?"

"Liberated it," Hog said, grinning. "We sort of had to get away from a bunch of guys who were shooting at us."

Stone asked, "What about the C.I.A.? If Leech is gone, will we be assigned someone else?"

"I'll see to it. The machinery is turning now. We may have some info by morning. Call me but use a public pay phone and no names . . . except mine. If we have to meet, don't all three of you come. I should have the passports by tomorrow night. I'll bicycle to Kiev Station at about eight P.M. and pass them to you. Okay?"

"Okay."

"Right. Take me back within a mile or so of the embassy. I bicycle all the time. They're used to it by now. Anything else?"

"News of Lee Daniels."

"I'll pass on anything I hear, but don't expect much. The K.G.B. has undoubtedly put him in a safe place, and they've got lots of secret holes."

Loughlin turned off the prospekt and halted in a shadowy side street. Hog unlatched the back door of the van, jumped out, and handed the bike down.

Davison got out and put a leg over the bike. "Don't take any wooden kopecks." He pedaled off.

They found the safe house after half an hour's looking. It turned out to be an apartment over a food store. The stairs were in the back. There was a fenced lot where they parked the van so it couldn't be seen from the street. It would be reported stolen, of course, but they would take a chance with it another day.

The apartment had two rooms, a living room–bedroom and a tiny kitchen. It was not much larger than one of the cubicles assigned them at the embassy. The bed would hold two of them. They flipped kopecks to see who would sleep on the floor.

There were canned goods on shelves, and bottles. They made a meal of sorts with vodka and went to sleep.

Rima Suslov was at the door early. She had a large knitted bag containing french bread, fruit, and a melon. "Hi," she said in flawless American, when Stone came to the door. "I'm Rima. Can I come in?"

"Absolutely," Stone said, taking the bundle. He eyed her with admiration. She was smallish, wearing dark pants, a long coat with a fur collar, a knitted red scarf, and a wool cap. Her face was round and smiling with bright blue eyes.

Loughlin whistled when he saw her, and she grinned at him.

Hog made her a bow, "Y'all's pretty enough t'be from Texas, sweetheart."

"I was born in Colorado, actually."

"What a shame," Hog said. "Well, we'll overlook that."

She doffed the wool cap and took off the coat. She

wore a modest blue sweater underneath. "So you're the three magicians who're going to get Lee Daniels out of the lion's den."

"With your help," Stone said.

"All right, but first things first. I haven't had breakfast."

"Neither have we." Hog went into the kitchen and began to rattle pans.

Rima asked, "Have you a plan?"

"We haven't seen the C.I.A. man yet . . . Jim Leech."

She frowned. "There's a rumor that Leech has been detained."

Loughlin asked, "What's that mean, detained?"

"It could mean anything. But it's only a rumor. I work with the C.I.A. off and on. What have you done about Yuri Rybak?"

"Who the hell is Yuri Rybak?"

She cocked her head at them. "He's the K.G.B. man whose job it is to keep tabs on the American press corps. Didn't they tell you at the embassy?"

Stone shook his head. "I guess they were leaving that for Leech. So what about Rybak?"

"He will probably know what happened to Lee Daniels."

"Ahhh," Loughlin said, drawing the sound out.

"Where can we find him?"

She made a face. "That is a problem. He frequents several bars I know about . . . But beyond that I don't know."

"What does he do in the daytime?"

She shrugged. "He has an office. I suppose he'd be there. But you wouldn't be able to get anywhere near it. Do any of you speak Russian?"

"Hardly any," Loughlin said. *"Da* means yes, huh?"

She laughed.

Stone inquired, "So we wait for nightfall?"

Rima nodded. "We wait. I hear you stole a van."

"Only borrowed it," Hog yelled from the kitchen. "Who wants to eat?"

# Chapter Six

Loughlin went out after dark and stole a pair of license plates and put them on the van.

Rima took them, in the van, to the Café Zarev where, she said, it was known that Yuri Rybak often hung out. He was a nasty little man, she told them. She had met him once. He pawed her and promised her a pair of fur-lined Italian boots if she would come to his apartment. She declined.

"But I would have liked to have the boots," she said wistfully.

"We'll find some for you," Hog promised.

The cafe was run by a Ukrainian, a big, beefy man; it was composed of a dozen tables and a bar. There was also a tiny little stage by the bar where an overdressed woman appeared and sang Ukrainian songs with much clapping of hands. She was accompanied by two musicians who looked very sad throughout.

They stayed for two hours but Yuri Rybak did not show.

Leaving the café an hour before midnight, they took Rima home. Stone walked into the building with her. "Ask your C.I.A. friends to get some weapons to us."

"I will ask." They walked into a hall that smelled of cooked food and tobacco. Rima took out a key and unlocked a door. As she opened the door a white square of paper stared up at them.

She picked it up. "It's from Jim Leech."

Stone looked at the paper. "It doesn't say so."

"It's a code. This is his code mark." She pointed to a curious figure that was not a letter. "It's in Russian; it says he will meet me tonight."

"Then I'll stay and meet him."

She shook her head. "If you leave the van in front of the building someone will report it. Go back to your rooms and I will send him there."

She tore the note in half and handed him one of the halves. "I'll give Jim the other half. That way you can be sure it's him."

He pocketed the paper. "It must be a dream to live in Russia."

She smiled. "This is my last year. They promised that next year I can go back to Denver." She glanced along the hall. "Now hurry up. You mustn't be seen here."

He patted her cheek and went out to the van.

Jim Leech arrived in an hour, presenting them with the other half of the note. He was an iron-gray-haired man in a fur *shapka* and a fur-necked coat. He came in, doffing the hat, and Stone made the introductions.

He said, "We were afraid you were in jail."

Leech shook his head. "I was not exactly arrested,

just detained for a bit. They explained to me very politely that some papers were not in order and it would take a day or so to correct them. They required me to stay and answer some questions—all very politely."

"While they sent someone to impersonate you."

"Apparently that's what happened."

Loughlin asked, "How could they know—"

"The bug war," Leech said. "The American Embassy is constantly fighting the war of the listening devices.

"But all in all it's worked out well, hasn't it? Rima told me about the trouble at Kiev Station. So it's probably good you never went back to the embassy. They'd have surrounded you as soon as you left it, if you had."

Hog said, "I reckon we're number one on the Russian wanted list."

Leech smiled. "So are a lot of other people. We'll see that you move to a new location every day or so. They won't get a line on you . . . if you're careful." He smiled again. "The fewer K.G.B. men you shoot, the better."

"Well of course they get in the way now 'n' then," Hog said casually. "Can you get us some hardware?"

"Yes . . . handguns. Rima says you went looking for Yuri Rybak tonight. You looked in the wrong place. Rima is a nice girl and may not know about Rybak's bad habits. The government doesn't like to admit it, but there are hookers in Russia." Leech jotted down an address and handed it to Stone. "This is a house of ill repute. That's what my old man used to call them in Utah. You can find Rybak there several times a week. I'll get you a photo of him. He's a slimy-looking little pig."

Stone said, "Our Russian is poor to nonexistent. How'll we get in the door? Or should we wait for him outside?"

"I'd say get him outside. We're short-handed or we would have done it long ago. Also, we know them and they know us—that's why you three can do this particular job better than we can. Make the sonafabitch talk, then you can do what you want with him. Personally I'd string him up by the balls and leave him, but then I'm known for my sweet nature."

"Does the K.G.B. know about Rima?"

"We don't have any indication that they do. But as soon as we think so we'll get her out of the country. We have a number of people in her position. The Russkis can't watch them all even though they try like hell to watch everyone. Stay away from the old women who sweep the streets. They'll report you for spitting on the sidewalk and make it sound like you took a shot at the General Secretary."

Stone asked, "D'you know where Rybak lives? It might be easier to get him there."

"Yes, we do—and no, it won't." Leech took out a narrow cigar case and selected a cheroot. He scratched a match and lighted it, blowing smoke. "He lives in a fort. Impossible to get in unless you're K.G.B., too. He does have a country house somewhere, as most of the big shots do. No, the whorehouse is the best place to grab him."

"When can we get us some weaponry?" Loughlin asked.

"One of my boys, Larson, is rounding them up now. He'll bring them here tomorrow." Leech took out the torn paper Rima had given him. "He'll show you this so you'll know who he is."

"Good show."

"You'd best lie up during the day."

"We will," Stone said. "And we'll go look for Rybak when it gets dark."

Leech's "boy" turned out to be a middle-aged man, very Russian-worker-looking in shabby clothes and a dirty gunnysack over his shoulder.

He gave Stone the torn bit of paper and came into the room. "I'm Charlie Larson, your Moscow gun dealer. I understand you guys are starting a new revolution."

He pulled a thick roll of cloth from the sack and unwrapped it on a table. It contained two Walthers and a .45 Colt automatic with boxes of ammo.

Hog examined the .45. "No silencers?"

"Too bulky," Larson said. "Learn to like the noise." He fished in his pockets. "I've got a new address for you. The boss suggests you move tonight."

"All right."

"He also suggests you get rid of the van. Park it somewhere in a nice public place and forget it."

"Wilco," Stone agreed. "Will you see that Rima knows where we've moved?"

"Hell, the C.I.A. can handle that, sure." Larson had a strip of newspaper and handed it over. "That's a photo of Yuri Rybak, taken a few weeks ago at a committee meeting. Study it, then burn it. Okay?"

"Right."

Rybak was not a handsome man. In fact, he looked like a furtive weasel in a dark suit. Stone handed it around.

Larson gathered up his gunnysack and went to the door. "Well, see you guys in the funny papers."

"When'll we see Jim again?"

Larson shrugged. "I dunno. He'll show up—or one

of us will. We'll contact you probably every day. If you need us, call Davison."

"How'll we know who's who?"

Larson grinned. "Okay. The code word is—what's a good code word?"

"Geronimo," Hog said.

"Geronimo it is." Larson grinned at them and went out.

Loughlin closed the door after him. "So we need new wheels. There's an architectural museum down the street. Why don't I take the van down there and swap it for something else?"

"Don't get a convertible," Hog said.

Loughlin looked at him. "There isn't a convertible in all of Russia! I doubt if they know what one is."

"As soon as it gets dark," Stone said.

They cleaned the new weapons and loaded them, then got some sleep. The day drifted by. Loughlin went out well after dark and drove the van across the river, found a lot with several dozen parked cars, and left the van in amongst them. A dark blue Mercedes caught his eye. He used a length of wire to open the door, slid inside, and hot-wired it deftly.

In less than an hour after leaving he was back with the Mercedes and parked it in the same lot off the street. The others were delighted with it.

The address of the whorehouse was off Tagansky Square and they drove there an hour before midnight. The establishment was in a large block of apartments, a slab-sided building, gray in the gloom, with only a few glimmering lights in windows. There were other cars on the street and Loughlin parked behind a shrouded truck.

Stone went inside to check the door. The cathouse was off an ell, a corridor that did not go through to the back of the building. When he put his ear to the door he could hear music; it sounded like western-style jazz.

He walked back to the main corridor, debating where the best place to wait for Rybak might be. As he paused in the hall, a door slammed and a man wearing a rumpled suit and a fur hat came out and stopped suddenly, seeing him. The man said something in Russian.

Stone turned as if he hadn't heard, and hurried toward the front door.

The man yelled at him. Stone glanced over his shoulder and pushed on the door. The man was drawing a pistol from under his coat. He was red-faced in anger. Another man appeared in the doorway behind him.

The man was about to fire at him. Stone yanked out the .45 as he threw himself flat. Instantly a round smashed the glass of the door over his head.

Stone fired twice and saw the man whirled around and shoved back violently into the second man, who began yelling.

Stone's third bullet made dust fly from the heavy coat and both men were hurled back into the room, the sharp sounds of the heavy automatic echoing in the hallway.

Jumping up, Stone pushed through the door and ran for the Mercedes. Loughlin had it fired up when he heard the first shots. It was moving slowly as Stone sprinted toward it and piled in.

A half dozen shots followed him, all wild. Some rapped into the truck ahead of them. Loughlin sped away and a man ran into the street far behind them and emptied a pistol. None of the shots came near.

Loughlin tooled the car around the next corner as the tires screamed.

Hog asked, "What happened? Didn't you like the girls?"

Stone grunted. "Rybak's got bodyguards. Bastard took a shot at me when I didn't answer him."

"Impolite not to answer folks," Loughlin said. "Is anyone on our tail?"

Hog turned. "Not yet."

Loughlin gave the car the gas on a long stretch and in a moment Hog said, "Lights behind us. Somebody's coming."

Loughlin adjusted the rearview mirror. "Coming fast, too."

Hog leaned out and aimed carefully. The Walther spat when he squeezed the trigger, once, twice, three times. But nothing happened; the pursuing car continued to gain.

Loughlin took a corner on two wheels. The car fishtailed when it came down but the Briton controlled it and fed it the petrol. They gained a hundred yards on the other.

"Get the hell off this street," Stone said. "They've got a faster car." He looked back at the corner. "The guy's a good driver, too."

They had turned into a wide boulevard. Loughlin took the next corner, hardly slowing down. Tires shrieked and Hog and Stone held on for dear life. Loughlin straightened the car and suddenly slowed. He yanked the wheel over and slammed on the brakes. The car came to rest in a small cul-de-sac. He cut the lights.

In a moment the pursuing car shot by, accelerating.

Loughlin backed out immediately, without lights, and spun the wheel, heading back the way they had come.

They had gone less than a hundred yards when a

second car came round the corner in a screaming turn. The car passed them as someone shouted and a shot hit the side of the Mercedes.

"Damn!" Stone said. "They saw we were running without lights."

The second car skidded as the brakes were slammed on. It stopped and began to turn as Loughlin made the corner as fast as he dared.

They were in a very narrow, dark street, so narrow he had to twist and turn to avoid carts and wagons that were parked helter-skelter alongside a high fence. Loughlin swore as he navigated the street, speeding up and braking.

They were two blocks away before lights appeared behind them. Loughlin switched off the lights and made a fast turn, switching them on again.

This time they lost the pursuer. Two turns later, Loughlin headed for their rooms. They were not followed.

The Mercedes had at least one bullet hole in the side.

"Ditch the car," Stone said. "Let's not take a chance of some cop stopping us."

"I'll drop you off and go on a mile or so," Loughlin said.

Stone fished out the new address and they stopped to pore over a map. When they located it, the address was an apartment building. It was only a three-story, very old and gray block that looked to be held up by the paint. It smelled terrible in the halls but the room itself was clean.

"It's better'n a tent," Hog observed.

Stone looked through the kitchen, a tiny alcove hidden by a flowered curtain. "The larder's not stocked."

"We're going to starve to death?"

"Unless somebody goes to the store . . . and none of us can."

"We could pretend to be deaf and dumb and just point to what we want," Hog suggested with mock brightness.

Stone laughed. "No chance. Best to call Davison and tell him our troubles."

Loughlin returned after parking the Mercedes several miles away. He'd had to lay low several times while militiamen in cars and jeeps cruised the neighborhoods. "More than usual, mates. You think they're looking for somebody?"

"Can't imagine who," Hog said complacently.

Rima showed up at noon the next day, smiling and cheerful. She turned wide-eyed and bit her lip when she heard about the car chase. "You could all have been killed!"

"But we weren't." Stone showed her the empty shelves. "How about doing some shopping for us?"

"Of course."

"I'll go along with her and carry it," Hog volunteered.

"You look less like a Russian than Santa Claus," Stone grunted. He took a coin and pointed to Loughlin. "Call it."

He flipped and Loughlin said, "Heads."

"It's tails."

"Damn. I knew you'd use your two-headed coin."

"Always, if it's important." Stone took Rima's arm. "Shall we?"

# Chapter Seven

Lee Daniels had never before spent so much as a night in a cell like the one he was in. He spent an hour staring at the tiny window, where he could see a bit of sky. Cloud formations moved slowly across it.

When he looked down at the gray walls they seemed to close in on him, to squeeze the life out of him. If he stood in the center of the cell he could almost touch each wall with his extended hands. And it was silent. Were there no other prisoners on the row?

He put his ear to the heavy door. He could hear nothing.

Once a day the door opened and a tray was given him. The first day it contained some black bread, potato pie, and a tin cup of something that he decided must be tea. It was cold and tasteless.

A guard came for the tray in an hour. When Daniels talked to him, the man merely grunted. He took the tray, the spoon, and the cup and departed, slamming the door. The next day it was a different man . . . as friendly as the first.

When were they going to interrogate him? He began to look forward to it. At least he'd have someone to talk to. Of course being Russians they would believe nothing he said, but it would be company, and sounds.

He began to fear the eternal silence.

He tried to climb the wall to the high-up window, but it was impossible. The wall was smooth, no foot- or handholds. Once he heard an airplane, very far away. But that was all.

A man could go crazy in a tiny cell like this, locked away from the rest of humanity. God! What was his wife thinking? Probably the State Department was trying to reassure her, but Daniels knew they had no idea where he was.

He began to make marks on the wall. One for each day.


There was a queue at the farmers' market and Rima stood in line while Stone waited outside. It was better that way, she explained. If someone decided to talk to him it might get awkward. So he waited, well away from the others, pretending interest in passing traffic.

How should they go about finding Rybak? His bodyguards would be more alert after the death of two of them at the whorehouse. Stone smiled inwardly.

But Rybak probably wouldn't change his habits because of it. He might beef up the guard staff, but he would continue to visit the girls. Doubtless he had a favorite or two that he saw frequently.

However, Rybak was also in charge of the K.G.B. unit that kept tabs on the American press corps. Maybe there was a way to get to him in that regard. People formed habits . . .

When Rima came out of the market, arms full of food, Stone took most of it and they walked back to the apartment.

He asked her, "Where does the American press corps hang out?"

"Mostly at the Hotel Vilna. You want me to find out?"

"Yes. We want to know if Rybak goes there."

"That sounds easy. I'll ask the bartenders."

Hog and Rima went into the kitchen and discussed dinner. Hog wanted chili and beans, but there was no Russian equivalent, not even for kidney beans, and nothing could be counterfeited. Rima prepared an egg dish, which was well received, and after supper she left to go to the Vilna.

Loughlin went out well after dark and returned in less than an hour with a Fiat, saying he had pushed it out of a garage into an areaway and started the engine there.

Hog suggested he could become a famous car thief when they returned to civilization.

Rima was back sooner than they expected with the info: yes, Rybak often hung out at the Hotel Vilna, not in the bar, but upstairs in some of the rooms.

"I think he gambles there," she said. "One of the bartenders told me there's a poker game going most of the time and Rybak loves to play."

"Does he win?" Loughlin asked.

"The bartender said that sometimes the American reporters let him win."

"How about any particular nights?" Stone said.

"Yes, I asked that. He's there almost every Monday."

Stone smiled. "Then that's when we'll lay for him. Rima, draw us a plan of the hotel."

She sat at a table and sketched the floor plan. "The hotel is occupied by foreigners, no Russians at all except the help. It's five stories high with a basement for automobiles and an alleyway for removing trash and bringing in supplies. There's a restaurant and a bar with a dance floor."

"Where're the poker parties held?"

"The bartender said 'upstairs.' I didn't ask him which floor."

"Wait a sec," Stone said. "If the hotel is only for foreigners, well, we're foreigners. We can go in and speak English there, right?"

"Certainly," Rima said.

"Okay. We'll be journalists. We'll go looking for the famous poker party."

"What do journalists talk about?" Loughlin asked.

"Wimmen," Hog said. "What you think?"

Rima laughed. "There'll be K.G.B. agents around. Do they know what you look like?"

"Davison said they took pictures of us when we came through Customs." Stone scratched his chin. "Now they're looking for us because we're not at the embassy, and they probably know we had something to do with the affair at the Kiev Station."

"Then don't hang out in the bar," Rima advised. "That's where the K.G.B. will be."


Stone called the embassy from a public telephone and talked to Davison, asking for a room or a suite at the Vilna Hotel. Davison promised to see to it.

"I'll send Jerry Gregg to make the arrangements and he'll get back to you."

"Who's Gregg?"

"An assistant. Look for him, okay?" He described Gregg.

"You got it." Stone hung up and went back to the room. Rima had left and Hog was asleep. Loughlin was playing solitaire. He told Loughlin what Davison had said; then he made himself comfortable and drifted off to sleep.

He woke instantly when someone rapped lightly on the door. Loughlin got up like a cat, a Walther in his hand. He touched Hog and, glancing at Stone, moved to the door. "Yes?"

A voice said, "Geronimo."

Hog was awake, the big .45 cocked in his hand, pointed at the door. Loughlin opened it silently and pulled a young man in.

"I'm Jerry Gregg!"

Stone told the others, "He's Davison's assistant." He went across the room and shook hands, then introduced Hog and Loughlin. Gregg watched them put away the artillery.

"Man, you guys come prepared!"

Hog said, "Don't fuck with us, baby, or we'll make you eat your grits."

Gregg laughed. "Okay." He held up his hands. "I surrender."

Stone asked, "What've you got for us?"

"They didn't have a suite, but I got a nice big room at the hotel for you. It's in the name of Harry Willis. Which one of you is Harry?"

Loughlin pointed to Stone. "He is. Who am I?"

Gregg shrugged. "A friend of Harry's. Harry is a newspaperman with the Louisville *Democrat* . . . if anyone asks. You won't have to show papers because we have a deal with the manager, all under the table of course. With the agreement that you won't cause any police trouble in the hotel."

"Trouble!?" Hog said in surprise. "Us?"

"What's the room number?" Stone asked.

"Three-twenty-two," Gregg said, handing him a key. "You won't have to go to the desk for it. Are you going to move in there?"

"We'll talk about it. Maybe."

"Okay." Gregg went to the door. "Anything else, just ask." He opened the door and went out.

"Nice quick work," Loughlin said. "That embassy really hauls ass."

Stone put the key in his pocket. "We can take a look at the room tonight."

It was well after dark when they went outside to the car. But the Fiat was gone. Loughlin frowned. "I left it right here."

Stone peered around; the street was empty except for a few parked cars. Was that a man's shadow in the doorway across the street?

He said to Hog, "Move back into the house as if we're going back into the room."

Loughlin slipped the Walther onto his hand. "There's someone off to the left."

"Act casual," Stone said softly. He followed them inside the big front door and closed it. There was a bar that slid across in a groove. He locked it and hurried after Hog, wondering if they'd surrounded the house.

Hog paused by the back door. There was an un-shielded bulb over the door, which he unscrewed. Opening the door, he peered out into the dark areaway.

He closed the door again. "I hear someone—you want to chance it?"

"K.G.B.," Stone said. "The house is surrounded. They probably just moved the Fiat a minute before we came out. Let's try the roof."

"Good show," Loughlin agreed.

"With any luck they'll try the room first." Stone led the way to the stairs and went up three at a time.

How the hell had the K.G.B. gotten onto them? Another listening device in the embassy? Had he mentioned where they were staying? No, he hadn't. Maybe they had followed Gregg.

He opened the door to the roof and stepped outside. It was a cold, crisp night with high clouds toying with a half-moon.

There was no one on the roof. Ventilation pipes and chimneys were everywhere, amid clotheslines, but nothing moved and it was very quiet.

He walked to the edge of the roof and looked at the next building. It was about five feet away. He gazed down into darkness. A radio or television set was playing somewhere in the chasm.

"Let's jump across," he said.

Loughlin stood on the parapet. "I'll go first." He jumped it easily. No shot came seeking him. Hog followed and, with a last glance around, Stone jumped.

They walked to the street side and looked over. A truck had just arrived and men were spilling out. An officer directed them around the building.

Stone said, "Let's get the hell out of here." He jogged across the roof.

It was a long building and at the far end they peered at the ground, seeing no one. The militia hadn't gotten this far yet.

They went downstairs in a hurry and out the back.

The first shot came as they climbed a board fence. The shot splintered a board just inches from Hog's head. Instantly a bright ray of light flooded the areaway and more shots followed.

Loughlin was first over the fence and he hissed at them, "This way—"

They were in a fenced yard filled with barrels, boxes, and cans of trash awaiting the hauling man. They had to fight their way across it. Men were climbing the fence behind them, shouting orders in Russian.

The beam of light caught them for an instant as they jumped down behind the cans, and a fusillade followed, ripping and shredding the metal cans just above them.

Hog rolled to one side and came up with the Walther leveled. He fired five quick shots and the light went out as someone screamed.

"Got the bastard," Hog said.

They ran between two buildings to the next street and across it. As they ducked into the shadows a truck came roaring around into the street and braked with a screech. Men piled out and ran to the building they had just left.

"Wish I had a goddamn Uzi," Loughlin said.

"We're fightin' a one-sided war," Hog agreed. "They got all the firepower."

"Shut up and make tracks," Stone said. "Those guys mean business."

The street contained a row of smaller houses and lights were going on as people heard the shots. To be safe they would have to get completely out of the area.

Loughlin looked up at the front of one building. "Gimme a boost up," he said to Hog. "I think I can reach the roofline."

Hog laced fingers together and Loughlin stepped into

them; Hog tossed him up easily. Stone followed, and he and Loughlin pulled Hog up. They were on a sloping roof that slanted down to within five feet of the ground on the far side. They jumped off into a garden, stepped across it, and came out on a narrow pathlike alley, too narrow for an automobile.

Listening, they could hear only the sounds of heavy trucks and a few distant shouts.

"Now what?" Hog asked, voicing all their sentiments.

If they called Davison, the listening devices might be attached to Russian ears.

"We hole up somewhere," Stone said—and looked upward. A helicopter came swooping in with searchlights blazing.

# Chapter Eight

In front of them was a long shed, and they dived into it as bullets spanged off the hard ground and shredded the eave of the shed. Running hard, they headed for the end of the building fifty yards away. They were undercover; the helicopter could only guess which way they'd gone. It was tearing up the roof, smashing and rending it with a torrent of bullets.

At the end of the shed was a path between houses, weedy and twisting. There were two searchlights on the helicopter and both were playing back and forth nervously, trying to pick them up. Stone snapped his fingers and pointed, and Loughlin ducked into the path, followed by Hog. Waiting till the searchlights swung away, Stone left the cover of the roof and ran hard.

But the gunship moved faster and the lights swung back.

Someone with an AK was firing directly down at

him. Stone slid to a halt as bullets pounded the path a yard ahead of him.

Then suddenly the marksman in the chopper threw up his arms and disappeared. His rifle fell into the night. Stone ran like a deer as one of the searchlights suddenly shattered. The helicopter lifted with a roar and gained height as it turned away.

He came upon Hog and Loughlin, both leaning on a slab of concrete, aiming pistols into the sky. Hog said, "Howdy, friend. You come to join up?"

Stone grinned at them. "Get moving, dammit. Now they know exactly where we are."

He led the way into the street. It was lined with apartments and a number of people were standing on steps. Someone yelled at them, probably, Stone thought, asking a question.

A chopper came overhead, a good distance up, and a searchlight switched on, beginning to quarter the ground. Stone hissed, "Into the first house!"

Everyone else moved into the houses hurriedly so they were not singled out. In the distance they could hear trucks roaring toward them, doubtless bringing militiamen . . . and police.

They ran through the house and Loughlin said, "We need a car! We'll never get away unless we find a car."

Hog said, "They'll shoot at a car soon's it moves!"

Stone stepped out into the dark. "We've got to keep going. They'll have more choppers and men here in a minute."

They were in an apartment complex with seven- or eight-story buildings built in a pattern around a parklike area. There were swings and slides and other children's playground equipment, some sheds, and a line of small buildings that looked like garages. And under one of the sheds were bicycles.

Stone grabbed one. He pulled it out and swung his leg over. "Here's the ticket!" He pedaled away as Hog and Loughlin yanked bicycles from the rack and followed.

Stone led them straight through the complex, staying under trees or running near walls. A chopper swung their way and he halted instantly, throwing the bike down and lying flat under a group of small trees. The searchlight did not touch them.

The chopper turned back and was joined by another.

"They don't think we got this far," Stone said, watching the searchlights playing down over an area a quarter of a mile away. "Let's get scarce."

They went on in single file, into the next street, a wide boulevard.

Loughlin stole another car, this time an ancient Zhiguli, a small car modeled after the Italian Fiat. They crowded in and Loughlin drove off sedately through the dark streets of Moscow.

The Vilna was in a busy section; there was much night traffic and no trucks at all. They put the car on a side street and strolled separately to the hotel.

There was a fancy-uniformed doorman who was tending a Chaika limousine as Stone approached. He walked into the ornate lobby, glancing around as if expecting someone. He saw Hog entering the bar and Loughlin standing by a kiosk, reading an American newspaper.

They had all examined the photo of Rybak again, before destroying it. Stone was sure he would know the man anywhere.

The first order of business was finding out about the poker party. A well-dressed, portly man was standing near the door reading an English-language newspaper. Stone asked him, "Where's the poker game tonight?"

The man looked at him and said in undoubted British, "Really, old boy, haven't the foggiest."

Stone went on and in a few moments Hog came out of the bar and motioned to him. "The party's upstairs in two-oh-three. They're talking about it in the bar. I don't think Rybak's here yet."

"Let's go look at the layout."

They walked to the stairs casually and Loughlin folded his paper and followed slowly. Room 203 was at the far end of the hall. The door was standing open and a few men were talking by the door, obviously telling jokes. Stone went past them into the room, nodding to others who only glanced at him. It was a large room with two green-felt-topped tables and men sitting around them in shirtsleeves. Two games were in progress. Yuri Rybak was not in evidence.

There was a bar with a man in a red vest behind it, talking to two customers. The scene might have been a Chicago hotel room, Stone thought.

He strolled back to the hall. Hog and Loughlin pretended to be interested in the paper. Stone shook his head slightly.

The joke tellers drifted into the room and Stone walked to the end of the hall. It turned at right angles; one set of steps went down, one went up. There was no window at the end of the hall. Hog and Loughlin came up beside him.

Stone said, "Let's see where this goes." He ran down the steps lightly to the next floor and two men came along in work clothes, pushing a cart piled high with refuse. He watched them take it out a rear door into a dark alleyway.

Stone stepped outside. There were two small trucks and several cars parked there. Beyond them was a shed with a steeply slanting roof.

Loughlin said, "Wonder if he'll come in this way . . . I mean, does he want it generally known that he gambles here with foreigners?"

Stone scratched his chin. "Maybe not . . ."

"Damned convenient," Hog said. "Up the stairs and into the room."

Stone nodded. It was damned convenient. So much so that it was very unlikely that Rybak hadn't noticed it. "Okay, let's bring the car around and park it here close by. When Rybak shows up we'll toss him in the trunk and take off. Right?"

"Right-o," Loughlin said. "I'll get the car." He ran up the stairs.

"He'll have bodyguards," Hog reminded Stone. "A couple at least."

"We'll just have to take them out." There were steps down to the ground level. He went down and walked back and forth looking at the space. There was room for half a dozen or more cars. An alley ran each direction for service vehicles. This was probably a very busy area for trucks during the day.

Where could they take Rybak? Maybe Loughlin should liberate another van. They could talk to Rybak in it, and show him the error of his ways—if he did not eagerly divulge the information they needed.

In a short while Loughlin returned with the Zhiguli and parked it in an area of deep shadow. Hog and Stone got in and they waited.

And waited. But Rybak did not show.

Every hour one of them walked upstairs to the poker room to look around, just in case. But no Rybak.

Hog said finally, "He's at the whorehouse getting laid. He'll be here tomorrow."

When Loughlin made a last check of the poker room he talked idly to one of the men at the bar and learned that Rybak did indeed show up frequently, but usually after ten in the evening. He then stayed until two or more. He was not considered a good player—or a good loser. He would moan and whine when he lost, the man said.

Stone called Davison from a pay telephone asking for another safe house. Davison agreed to meet him in an hour with a key. "I'll take the Metro to Durov Street."

They drove there at once and waited across the street from the Metro entrance, in front of a cemetery. When Davison appeared, Stone hurried across to meet him.

Davison asked, "Why didn't you use the room at the Vilna?"

"Because we're edgy about bugs in the embassy. Does anyone know you're meeting us tonight?"

Davison shook his head. "I told no one."

"Good. Right after Gregg came to us with the hotel key we had a regiment of K.G.B. types breathing down our necks. It's making us a little paranoid about trusting anyone. How well do you know Gregg's background?"

"He's been checked and rechecked for security clearances, the same as all of us. Do you think he had anything to do with it?"

"It's curious, that's all. Does Gregg know about Rima?"

"No. I only know because Jim Leech and I have worked on a few projects together and one of them involved her."

"Please don't let Gregg know then. And maybe you'll want to check him again."

Davison made a face. "All right."

"It could be life and death."

"I hear you." Davison nodded. "I'll get the machinery moving in the morning. Are you any closer to Daniels?"

"I think so. We have a plan."

The other put up a hand. "Don't tell me about it. I might talk in my sleep."

Stone grunted, "I wasn't going to."

He watched Davison return to the Metro and walked back across the street as it began to rain lightly.

## Chapter Nine

*Pravda,* which is a Russian newspaper, and the Russian word for *truth,* printed a short article concerning Lee Daniels, journalist.

Mr. Daniels had apparently been abducted by persons unknown for their own secret purposes, and though the Moscow police, aided by other interested organizations, had searched diligently for him or for some evidence of him, they had turned up nothing. The newspaper declared it was deplorable that such a thing could happen. The agencies would not give up but would continue to search.

Daniels marked off the days, deciding on a ritual; he would mark the wall each morning when he woke. He had felt a temptation to make the mark on the evening before, then found himself making two marks for the same day.

It was a measure of the importance of things. The

second most important thing of the day was the hour,
never quite the same, when he would receive his food
tray. He tended to think of things before or after the
food tray . . . the dividing point. He also saved bits of
bread to eat later. It was coarse, hard bread, the worst
he had ever eaten, but he savored it, as much for the
ritual of eating as for nourishment.

He still attempted to speak to the men who brought
the trays, but was never successful. At best he received
a grunt in reply.

And he found himself speaking aloud many times,
expressing one thought or another. He was glad to hear
the sounds. Occasionally he sang to himself, and sometimes he would sit and try to remember the names of all
the songs he had ever heard, and speak them aloud.

No one came to interrogate him.

He decided they were breaking him down by leaving
him alone in a silent cell, a tiny cubicle with its tiny
patch of sky. Wasn't that something like the Chinese
water torture, one drop on the forehead at a time, over a
period of time . . . ?


A Russian civilian accosted Stone and his men the
next morning in the lobby on their way out. He spoke
passable English, saying he had learned it when he
served as a crew member of a Canadian ship for two
years. He had been in New York and in many southern
ports as a youngster, and was perhaps thirty-five. A
thin, slightly bowed, very poorly dressed man, he reminded Stone of a waiter in an all-night diner.

He began asking them if he might try out his English,
since he hadn't spoken it for several years. He sat between Hog and Stone and chatted for half an hour before he dropped his bomb.

"I hear you are looking for the American journalist, Lee Daniels. Perhaps I may be of assistance. My name is Vasili."

Stone almost grabbed him to shake him, but managed to restrain himself. He glanced at Hog, who was regarding the Russian as if expecting him to explode.

Hog said mildly, "Tell us where you heard that or I'll take you apart piece by piece and shove the parts up your ass."

Vasili looked startled. Then he smiled, spreading his hands. "I hear many things, my friends. It is my—how do you say—my stock in trade."

"Go on," Stone said.

Vasili looked uncomfortable. "I buy and sell information. It is the way I live." He indicated the lobby room with his hand. "I sell information to these gentlemen. Very few speak the language so I translate for them. I get them passes to this place or that, but mostly I sell information."

"And how do you connect us to Lee Daniels?"

"You are Americans. Daniels is an American." He shrugged elaborately. "So I put two and two together. Americans want to know what happened to Lee Daniels. Especially American journalists. Is it not so?"

Stone nodded. "All right. For the moment we'll accept that on face value. What do you know about Daniels?"

"I can tell you where he is."

Hog grinned. "Let's go outside for a little walk."

"No, my friend," Vasili said quickly. "I will stay here in the hotel surrounded by people." He edged away from Hog.

Stone said, "I expect you have a price?"

"Certainly. I told you, it is how I make my living.

You will give me the equivalent of five hundred dollars and I will tell you where to find Lee Daniels."

"Five hundred bucks!" Hog almost yelled. A few heads turned.

"Shhh," Vasili warned. "You must never say where you got the information! It would cost me my freedom."

"That's a lot of money," Stone told him.

"Perhaps, but I must get out of Russia. I will have to pay certain bribes to do this. I must return to Paris. My woman is waiting for me." He looked abject. "I have not seen her for a year."

Stone studied the Russian for a moment. Then he said, "You go take a hike, Vasili. Let us discuss it among ourselves. All right?"

"Of course. Of course." Vasili got to his feet, all smiles again. "You will call me, no?"

"We will call you, yes."

The Russian nodded and walked away.

Hog beckoned Loughlin, who had been talking to a Britisher, and the three settled themselves in a corner. Stone told Loughlin what Vasili had said. "He wants five hundred to tell us where Daniels is."

"Let me shake it out of him," Hog growled. "It'll only take a minute. I'll pull his head out through his asshole and he'll sing pretty as a French canary."

"How do we know he knows?" Loughlin said.

"A very good question. We don't."

"Then we shouldn't let him out of our sight till he proves up. Right?"

"Right," Hog said.

Thoughtfully, Stone said softly, "He says he's been selling info to the foreign press here in the hotel for a while, making a living at it. If so, Jim Leech should know him."

"Good show," Loughlin said, grinning. "Ask Leech." He glanced around. "There're phones over there behind those shrubs. Let's give him a call."

Stone rang the number Leech had given him, and the familiar voice came on the line. Stone said, "Geronimo."

"Hello Chief," Leech replied. "How's the tribe?"

"We've got a guy who may not have all his feathers. Maybe you know him. Skinny type says his name is Vasili. Makes his beans by peddling info. Is he on the up and up?"

"I doubt it," Leech said. "Take everything with a grain of sodium chloride. Yes, I know 'im."

"Has he ever been on the money?"

"Oh yes. He has to come through now 'n' then or no one would trust him again. It depends on what he's selling to you."

"Missing newsmen."

"Uh-huh. Take it with a large grain." Leach paused. "Of course, he *may* have the goods." He paused again. "I know I'm not much help, but that's the way it is."

"A judgment call."

"Right."

"Thanks." Stone hung up and went back to the others. He shrugged. "Leech knows the guy but doesn't trust him farther than he could throw a piano, left-handed. It's up to us."

Loughlin nodded. "Then we have to go along. But not for five hundred . . . not in advance."

Stone looked at Hog. "Agreed?"

Hog scratched his neck. "Not for five hundred."

They had another talk with Vasili. The Russian was all smiles, until they mentioned money.

"One hundred in advance, Vasili. And you come along with us to wherever it is."

"But I cannot do that!"

Hog smiled on him benignly. He slid a huge hand along the skinny Russian's shoulders. "You ain't got a hell of a lot of choice, little pal. Y'all aren't getting out of our sight."

Vasili turned pale. "I will yell for a policeman!"

"One half a yell is all you'll get," Hog promised. "Then I fold you up and put you in my pocket and we go out for a walk."

Vasili looked from one man to the other. Seeing no help in their eyes, he seemed to shrink. "You would not cheat me, would you?"

Stone shook his head. "No cheating, but you have to deliver."

"What does that mean, deliver?"

"If you lie to us you are in the soup." Stone saw the Russian blink in confusion. "If you lie to us you are dead."

"I tell you the truth! But I cannot go with you."

"Why not?"

Vasili hesitated. His eyes seemed to be seeking a way out. "I—I must be making plans—when you give me money I must prepare to go—I have people to see—"

"You've waited a long time now. You can wait a little longer."

Vasili deflated. He sank down, closed his eyes, and looked utterly miserable.

Stone thought, this guy is looking for an Academy Award for one scene. He glanced at the others. Hog shook his head. Loughlin made a face.

Stone said, "Okay, you get a hundred in advance. And you come along with us. When we find out where

Daniels is—and we can get to him, you get another two hundred."

Vasili looked up as though he had been stabbed in the heart. "Three hundred! Three hundred is all you'll pay!?"

"All it's worth," Hog said. "Where is Daniels?"

Dully: "Out of the city."

"Out of the city where?"

Vasili frowned at Stone. "Give me my hundred first."

Stone took out his wallet and counted out the rubles, handing them over. Vasili counted them again and tucked them into an inner pocket.

He looked at them, sighed, and said, "Daniels has been moved to a sanitarium outside Moscow."

"How far away?"

Vasili shrugged. "Forty, maybe fifty miles. I will get you a map. I have never been there."

"There's a sightseeing desk here in the hotel," Loughlin said. "They ought to have maps." He got up and strolled away.

Stone asked, "What else do you know about Daniels?"

"I know nothing about him at all. I have been told only that he has been moved. I do not even know where he was moved from."

"But is he alive."

"Oh yes, certainly."

"Why would they move him?"

Vasili looked at him in surprise. "I am only a poor man, not a powerful politician. How would I know why they do things?"

"Huuummm."

Loughlin returned in a few moments with a bright-colored map of Moscow and environs. It was in French.

He laid it in front of Vasili, handing him a pencil.

Vasili studied the paper for a moment, then drew a line. "This is the road you must take. It will go through a village called Amga. Outside the village you will see a sign that says the sanitarium is just beyond, a mile or two."

"And Daniels is in the sanitarium."

"Yes. It is not a large place ... but there will be guards."

"Why would they put him in a sanitarium?"

Vasili spread his hands. "How would I know?"


They let Vasili go into the bar and held a brief conference. If the man was telling the truth, he would wait for his two hundred dollars. If not, it didn't matter. Loughlin said, "We'll have to assume his info is correct —until we find it's not."

"And watch out for a trap," Hog declared.

"I wish we had some AKs. Can we liberate a few before we go?"

Stone shook his head. "Too chancy. But we'll need a van. Look around for one tonight."

# Chapter Ten

Loughlin found a van, only a year or so old, painted brown with no lettering on the sides. It had a number of empty wooden crates inside, which they hauled out and left on a dark street. There was a stack of packing blankets, so perhaps the van had been used to haul furniture or goods for sale.

Using Vasili's map, they took the marked road out of the city. Loughlin drove as usual, with Stone on the seat beside him and Hog in the back on a crate, leaning on the back of the front seat between them.

The road was fair to poor and they passed a dozen trucks. In half an hour Loughlin said, "I think we're being followed."

Stone peered at the back road, seeing nothing. "No lights."

"Somebody's back there, driving without lights. I can see a shadow now and then."

"Turn our lights out," Stone said.

"Wait'll we make a curve. Then he won't know if we've stopped or turned off."

"Right."

"If we're being followed," Hog said, "that ain't good."

Loughlin said, "If there was a place to pull over—we could let him go on by."

Stone nodded. The land wasn't flat, but in the clumps of trees they passed the van would probably stand out, even in the dark. Off to the right was a birch forest, but it was too far.

"Here's a curve," Loughlin said. The road curved to the left, down a slight slope, then straightened out again. The Briton switched off the lights as they began to straighten. "Will that fool anybody?"

"Maybe not. We must be more than halfway there . . ." Stone scratched his chin. "We might be smart not to let them join up—if that's what they have in mind."

"So you think Vasili sold us out?"

Hog said, "He told us the truth, didn't he? He said he sells info. So he sold some info to the K.G.B. Us."

Loughlin glanced at Stone. "I think Texas is right for once. It's a trap. They're in front of us and behind us."

"It's our move," Hog agreed.

"Okay, take the first road off." Stone pulled the .45 and took out the clip and put it back with a snap. He patted his pockets for the two spare clips.

When the road made a dip, Loughlin switched on the lights as they headed down. At the bottom he turned left abruptly. It was not a road, more a path, but he gave the van the petrol. "Hang on, chums—" They rocked over uneven spots but the van gained speed quickly, rolling over brown grass.

They were a mile or more along a gentle slope before Hog said, "The bad guys are behind us. I think they just turned off the road."

Stone grunted. "Let's hope they haven't got a radio with them to call for help." If not, they had divided the enemy force and now only had to face half of it—they hoped.

They crossed a field and suddenly a wood fence was before them.

Loughlin yelled, "Duck!" and the van crashed through.

The old, wooden fence splintered like matchsticks, doing no damage to the van. They went down a steep slope and found themselves in a grove of old trees, which spread along a fairly level stretch of ground. Loughlin navigated between the trees skillfully.

A stream appeared, wandering from the right, with trees and weeds along the banks. Loughlin swung the wheel and crossed water; the van bumped and splashed; then they went up a bare slope and along a rounded ridge.

Stone looked back. "How's the pursuit?"

"Don't see anything," Hog replied.

Stone studied his watch. "Probably about three hours till daylight. We'll have to leave the van then and get lost in the sticks."

Loughlin said, "We'll have to leave the van sooner than that, old boy." He braked and came to a halt, switching off the lights.

They climbed out to find themselves at the edge of a sheer drop. They had come along a ridge to the edge and probably could back the van in broad daylight, with help, but at night it was impossible.

And behind them they could see a glimmer of moving lights in the trees.

"Damn," Hog said, "wish we had us some grenades to booby-trap this here van with."

Stone led them down the hill, along the edge of the scarp, till they found a place to climb down, slipping and sliding to the bottom. They were in a wide sandy wash. Winter runoff had carved the hill over the centuries, eating away half of it and still working on the rest.

They crossed the wash and entered a small forest. At the edge they could make out flashlights on the ridge. The Bad Guys had reached the van.

"Council of war," Stone said. "We assume that this entire thing was a trap? Or is Lee Daniels really in the sanitarium, as Vasili said?"

"In a pig's eye," Hog said. "It was a trap from beginning to end."

"I tend to agree." Loughlin nodded quickly. "I'd guess it's a K.G.B. deal all the way, so why would they tell the truth about the sanitarium?"

Stone smiled. "You've convinced me." He glanced around. "We've got to find a place to hole up. They could bring choppers looking for us in the morning."

Hog Wiley said, "They'll figure we're heading back for Moscow, won't they?"

"Probably. And we are. What we need is transportation. Let's look for a farm."

Loughlin said reasonably, "If we stay in the forest the choppers won't find us."

Hog nodded and Stone hitched his belt and led out. "All right, let's make tracks."

They trudged north.

A helicopter passed overhead several thousand feet up. It droned out of sight and hearing.

"They looking for us," Hog said, smiling at the sky. "But they don't know where to look."

A few fixed-wing aircraft flew over, high up, but no one came near. Studying the map, Stone figured they were somewhere south of Moscow but not far from a well-traveled highway. If they went east they should come to it.

They walked between the dark tracings of trees whose upper branches were shrouded in fog, and when morning came it was a gradual lightening, so gentle that it was hardly noticed. There was no wind at all and the silence was a thousand miles deep.

But the fog burned away at last and the sun consented to shine again. The trail they followed curled away before them between high brush with trees laced overhead.

They were nearly surprised by the helicopter that came over a ridge and was atop them in an instant. They halted at once, standing stock-still, not looking up, and the chopper passed by—then swung around.

Stone yelled, "Into the trees!"

They jogged eastward through the trees. It was a dense forest that seemed primeval, as if no one had been through it since the beginning of time. This chopper zipped on by overhead, too.

Stone led for an hour, then Loughlin took over and they went on without stopping. In another hour Hog took the point, skirting grassy meadows, staying within the tree cover. Several times they halted to stand motionless, glued to tree boles, while aircraft skimmed overhead, engines droning angrily.

They ran all day long with short rest periods. A few

deer jumped, startled, as they approached, and rushed off. Birds squawked at them as they passed. Good signs, Stone thought.

One bad sign, too.

He grunted to the others, "We didn't pass the highway the map showed." He got out the map again.

Loughlin's finger traced a route toward the southeast. "We must have veered off and missed it."

"And maybe a good thing," Hog said. "By now they got forty thousand trucks on that road, loaded with militia."

Stone squinted at the far-off farm. "I wish to hell we had some binocs."

"Or some C rations," Hog added. "It gets hungry in these woods." He patted his huge chest. "A man like me gets weak and faint not eatin'."

Loughlin rolled his eyes.

Stone said, "I don't see any wires to that house—no poles. They probably have no phone or electricity."

"What're you thinking of?"

"Food."

Hog pointed. "There's some cows there, near the house. We could cut one up and fry us some steaks. Say, one cow for each of us."

"Helicopter," Loughlin snapped. "Down!"

They dropped into the grass under the fringe of trees. The chopper went over them fifty feet up and headed for the house, then swung south. They watched it disappear.

"It's nice not to be forgotten," Loughlin said.

They remained prone for a while but no other chopper came their way. Probably, Stone thought, the search was concentrating on another area. Since only one chopper had come here, maybe the Russians didn't think they'd come this far.

Continue to think that way, Ivan.

They headed across the fields to the farmhouse.

Two dogs came running at them, and Loughlin and Hog picked up heavy sticks. The dogs circled them, growling. Hog swatted one on the butt and he ran off howling. The other retreated, still growling and snarling. Loughlin ran at him with the stick and the dog scrambled, yipping, to get out of the way.

Stone led in a roundabout path to get close to the house. It was a log-and-board cabin that looked very stout. There were several outbuildings, chicken pens, and a pigsty. Alongside one of the buildings was a plow.

Cautioning the others to remain, Stone moved along the side of the house and looked around a corner. Ten feet away was an open door. Slowly he edged along the wall to the door from which came a delicious smell of stewing meat.

He looked around the door. He saw a tiny room that was obviously a kitchen. There was a black wood stove that took up most of the room with a box piled with wood sticks beside it.

On the stove a black iron pot was simmering.

Stone bit his lip. It smelled so goddamn good! He could hear voices in another room. A man was speaking rapidly, a woman answering with grunts. The voices sounded so close! The two could not be more than a few yards away.

Stone wadded up a handkerchief, stepped inside, and took hold of the handle of the pot. He was outside with it in half a moment, heading for the trees. The others saw him coming hurriedly and kept pace with him, each noting the iron pot.

They were in the edge of the trees close to the north side of the house before they heard the outcry. The farmers had discovered the theft of their supper. There was a good deal of shouting.

In ten minutes they were a good distance from the house, still in the woods. Stone put the pot down and they crowded around.

The stew was delicious.

# Chapter Eleven

The cell door opened suddenly with a clang. Lee Daniels had been dozing on the cot. The loud sound startled him, as if he had been shot. He rolled over, clutching the thin mattress, staring at the door. A man he had never seen before stood in the doorway, scowling at him. "You come."

"Come where?" Daniels sat up.

The guard growled, "You come."

Feeling tired, Daniels got up and straightened slowly. He was ninety years old. He took a halting step and the guard grabbed his arm, yanking him into the corridor.

"All right," Daniels said, "I'm coming."

The corridor was dim and dreary and smelled stale. The guard grunted and walked ahead of him, a strange-looking creature, one shoulder higher than the other, a scowling face, gray in color . . .

What now? Had they finally remembered he was here? Had the State Department managed to gain his freedom? God! How he wanted to see a New York paper.

He followed the lopsided guard through two heavy metal doors, which the man laboriously unlocked and locked again. At a third door a seated guard frowned at him, wrote something in a book and motioned them on.

They went down a hall to a doorway and inside. It was a small, stuffy room, very like a cell. There were a metal table and several chairs with a window on one wall that faced nothing. It was probably a one-way-glass affair. Daniels wondered who was behind it, staring at him.

The guard slammed the door behind him and Daniels sat down in one of the chairs, looking at the room. It was just as gray and colorless as his cell. Was everything in Russia gray? Why did people choose to live such gray existences?

Maybe they didn't know any better.

After a while the door opened and Colonel Zarnov entered. "Hello, Mr. Daniels." He sat at the table, hands folded on it.

Daniels nodded.

"Not talkative today?"

"Let me out of this fucking place!"

Zarnov smiled thinly. "Your anger is showing. You haven't enjoyed our hospitality?"

"You are pigs, the lot of you! You belong back in caves!"

Zarnov made a face. "An evil mood today, Mr. Daniels, and we are being so generous with you."

The anger welled up, impossible to control. Daniels jumped to his feet. "You are a lot of uncivilized primitives!"

"Shut up!"

"You are animals! You're no better than pigs in the goddamn mud, the bunch of you! You stink, Zarnov! This room stinks since you came in!"

"Shut your mouth or I will have you tied!" Zarnov pounded the table. "Sit down!"

Daniels leaned against the wall and closed his eyes. How did a man deal with shitheads like Zarnov? He let his breath out and sat wearily, staring at the Russian. "What do you want with me, Zarnov?"

"You have certain information which we must have. You know perfectly well what we want. Why not make it easier on yourself? I will supply you with pens and paper and you will write out what we wish and we will let you go."

"I don't believe anything you say."

The colonel shrugged. "I care nothing about that. It is not necessary for you to believe me. I ask you again. Will you write out what we wish?"

"I don't know anything of what you want. I am not a spy. I am a journalist doing his job and always have been."

"My dear Daniels. We know perfectly well that you supply the C.I.A. with information. It will not help your case to lie to us."

Daniels studied the other. Would it be possible for him to make up a lot of material out of whole cloth in order to get free? He could write out a ream of stuff—but would Zarnov believe any of it? He sighed. Probably not. The Russian was probably more knowledgeable about clandestine affairs than he. He could probably never fool Zarnov.

Zarnov said, "Time is important to us, Daniels. I will not allow you much more. Make up your mind you are going to give us what we ask."

"And if I did and could—you would kill me."

Zarnov registered astonishment. "Kill you? Certainly not! You would be handsomely paid and set free. I promise it. And no one would ever know."

"And my continued absence?"

"We would tell the press you have been making an extensive tour of Siberia and were in an area where there was no opportunity for communication with the outside world. I assure you there are areas like that. One of my staff will prepare pages of material for you to rework and give to your editors."

"You've thought of everything."

"Of course." Zarnov smiled. "We both get what we want and no one the wiser."

"Except me."

"If you are worried about the material, Mr. Daniels, I assure you our Russian writers are competent. You will receive material you could not otherwise get. Your editors will be very pleased."

Daniels shook his head.

"Come, come—don't be stubborn."

Daniels flared, "You don't understand anything! I will not do it! I will not! I will not!" He slammed his fist down on the table.

Zarnov rose instantly and went to the door. He glanced back as he opened it. "You are a fool." He went out and shut the door.

Immediately the same guard came in and pulled him up. "Come."

He was taken back to the cell and the heavy door slammed shut upon him.

At noon they halted at the edge of a long, shallow treeless valley that stretched away before them for several miles. The forest came down close on one side and a rugged hill on the other.

And as they sat, resting, a tiny movement caught Stone's eye. He pointed it out to the others. "Is that a vehicle there, in the valley?"

It was. The first of several vehicles. They came winding into the valley in single file and a chopper came floating above them.

"Jesus!" Hog said. "They decided to search this area!"

"Three trucks and two jeeps," Loughlin said, counting. "At least a hundred men."

"And a chopper. No, two choppers," Hog said as a second machine appeared far down the valley.

"It's nice to know we're so important," Loughlin observed. "When they shoot us we ought to get half a page in *Time* magazine."

The trucks, led by one of the jeeps, came on quickly, heading directly for them. They retreated into the forest as men spilled from the trucks and, at whistled orders, spread out in a long line to enter the trees.

All they could do was find places to hole up. Hog squirmed under a fallen log; Stone wormed his way into a thorny bush, finding a depression that he curled up in. Loughlin climbed a tree and hid himself in a clump of leaves. The line of militiamen went past and none of them looked up. A few poked at brush with bayonets but they were past quickly, probably bored with such duty.

Stone squirmed out and Loughlin dropped from the tree. Hog had to have a hand to get out, being wedged under the log. Looking at the line of vehicles, Stone said, "There's our transportation. How many guards would you say?"

"I see five or six," Loughlin said, shading his eyes.

The guards were gathered on one side of the line, in the shade. The two helicopters were droning over the forest, quartering it.

Stone beckoned and they approached the vehicles on the sunny side, walking casually. "Grab the jeep," Stone said. "It'll be fastest."

"Right-o." Loughlin grinned. "I'll swing it around and you blokes jump in."

There was no one near the jeep. It was Czech-made, they saw as they drew near. Loughlin swung aboard and started the engine. Stone and Hog leaned over the hood of the nearest truck, pistols in their hands. One of the guards looked around in surprise at the engine sound and began to run back toward the jeep.

Hog fired once, dropping him.

The other guards looked startled. The jeep swung in a tight circle and Stone jumped in the front, finding an AK-47 on the seat. He picked it up as Hog clambered in and Loughlin gunned it.

Bullets cracked over their heads as they sped down the line of trucks. Stone fired back with the AK and Hog fired at the second jeep, shredding a tire.

In a moment they were past the line of vehicles. Men ran out and knelt to fire after them. Stone used up the clip firing back and saw one man topple.

Then they were out of range.

Loughlin yelled, "I saw antennas. They'll call the choppers in a sec."

"Get the hell out of this valley," Stone called back.

"Too late," Hog said. "Chopper coming. Gimme the AK."

Stone passed it back to him. There was a box of spare clips on the floor. He handed Hog one.

In a moment Hog began firing. The chopper, painted a light green, swerved and lifted. Machine-gun fire spurted from it and Loughlin broke his course.

The helicopter was a bigger target and Hog was an accomplished marksman against aircraft. As he fired, pieces flew off the chopper. It swerved more violently. The tail rotor was suddenly smashed and the chopper fishtailed as Hog yelled in triumph, still pumping shots at it.

The forest was very near as the second chopper appeared.

Hog emptied the second clip and reached for a third as the green chopper, rocking violently, managed to land and swung around, smashing the big rotor as fire erupted. Stone saw men jump out and run; then they were in the trees.

Loughlin steered between tree trunks for another two hundred yards before he could go no farther. "That's all she wrote," he said, piling out. He lifted the hood and yanked at wires. Hog shredded the rear tires, then they ran after Stone.

The second chopper flashed over them at great speed, too low and too fast for a shot. They watched it turn and come back but it hadn't spotted them. They hugged trees and remained motionless as the chopper, this one blue and white, nosed about like a hound after a bone, firing a burst into suspicious clumps now and then.

As it moved away they went on quickly, bending

left. The Russkis must be fuming, Stone thought. One hundred men couldn't round up three. And two expensive choppers down! Well, both pilots had been a little foolish—or they had no idea who they were up against. Hog had been shooting at aircraft for years . . .

But the trouble was that now the Russians knew where they were; no need to beat the bushes elsewhere. They had to execute that well-known military maxim: get the fuck outa here.

The Red commander flung out a line of men, hoping to block their passage, and the three ran into it in a wild and steep gorge. Stone was leading when he ducked as he saw the glint of metal ahead. A shot came whanging past to richochet off a rock.

Stone rolled and pushed the .45 out ahead of him. He fired at movement and rolled again. To his right, Hog opened up with the AK, spraying hot lead into the brush, and someone wailed.

A whistle sounded and suddenly men sprang up and charged them.

Stone counted seven as he emptied the Colt, aiming carefully. Loughlin fired deliberately on his left and Hog caught them in a deadly crossfire.

All seven went down.

Stone picked up an AK as he moved forward. He shoved an extra clip under his arm and searched the gorge for others, finding none. They were through the line.

But the hot little firefight would bring reinforcements. He jogged up the gorge with Loughlin at his heels, also with an AK. The enemy was supplying them nicely.

Hog lagged behind and came up when Stone paused. "They ain't following."

"Smart," Stone said. He looked up as the chopper engine came close. But the pilot was staying higher, moving and circling, making it difficult for a sniper.

When it moved off, Stone led them up out of the ravine and continued eastward.

# Chapter Twelve

Vasili Anoprikov had a hundred dollars from the three Americans—and a few rubles from the K.G.B. He would get no more money from either. The K.G.B. was tight as virgin pussy and the three Americans were probably dead by now.

But the K.G.B. had given him a course of action. They had told him very little—only enough: that they knew three American mercenaries were seeking an American journalist named Lee Daniels.

That much they'd had to tell him. They had not told him the three were war-wise, streetwise, and extremely dangerous. "Frequent the foreign hotels," they said. "And if you find them, here's what you must do..." And they had outlined a plan. The mercenaries would be led down the garden path, surrounded, and shot to pieces. When they left Moscow, they would never be seen again.

Vasili thought about it when the money was nearly

gone. The K.G.B. outlined a plan that had no basis in reality. It was a trap, pure and simple.

Well, he knew about the American journalist. What if he made up some story or other and sold it to the American Embassy!

Wouldn't they be gullible too?

There had been no mention of the American Lee Daniels in Soviet newspapers—to his knowledge. So it must be a secret that would become his lever. If the American Embassy reacted at his mention of the name, then he would pursue it.

From a pay telephone he called the embassy and asked to speak to someone in charge.

A noncommittal voice asked him, "What is it regarding, please?"

"Lee Daniels," Vasili said.

He was surprised at the speed with which he was connected to someone. A voice said in his ear, "I am Leonard Schwartz. What is your name, please?"

"I am . . . Boris," Vasili said.

"All right, Boris. What can you tell me about Mr. Daniels?" Schwartz spoke excellent Russian. He had a deep, pleasant voice and Vasili imagined him to be a big, thickset man.

"I can tell you where Daniels is kept."

"When can we meet?" Schwartz asked.

Vasili was prepared for the question. "I want to sell the information, you understand."

"Ahhh. You want to sell it . . . That makes a difference, doesn't it?"

"Why should it?" Vasili said, slightly miffed. "You want to know, I want to sell. It is simple business. I am not a rich man, you understand. I have to sell what I can."

"All right. Let us meet and we will discuss details. Will Gorky Park do?"

Vasili thought a moment. "Yes. Along the river, by the Tretyakov end—do you know the gallery?"

"Yes. How will I know you?"

Vasili smiled. "We will both be holding folded newspapers under our left arms. Is that good?"

"Fine," said Schwartz. "In an hour?"

"Will you bring money?"

"I will bring money. Good-bye, Boris."

"Good-bye." Vasili hung up and stared out at the street. It was rather fun playing spy.

Schwartz called Davison's office and was told Davison was out with a fever. He was expected back in the morning. Would Mr. Gregg be able to help him?

"Mr. Gregg would do fine. Put him on."

Gregg came on the line, "Jerry Gregg here . . ."

"Leonard Schwartz, Jerry. I just took a call from a guy named Boris who claims to know where Lee Daniels is."

"Jesus! No kidding!"

"I didn't ask him many questions—didn't want to scare him off. He agreed to meet me, but this is not my slice of strawberry pie. You're better equipped to handle it."

"No problem, Leonard. Does he know you?"

"Not at all. You can say you're me, just for the meet."

"Fine. Tell me about what he said."

Schwartz outlined the conversation. He had promised no specific amount of money. He would carry a folded newspaper under his left arm.

Gregg smiled at that. He looked at his watch. "I'd better get going."

He went downstairs and got a car from the motor pool. He drove around the garden ring and crossed the bridge at the end of the park, then turned right and left the car in a lot at the far end of the park. It was getting dark.

He bought a newspaper and folded it as he walked toward the river. Music was playing from somewhere in the park to his right and he could hear children's voices. At the riverside he stood for several moments under the trees. Few people were about, most hurrying home before dark. He slipped the paper under his arm. He was wearing a dark overcoat and a fur hat; he looked like everyone else. He hunched his shoulders; it was getting chilly.

A thin young man came along the river walk with a newspaper under his arm. He looked closely at Gregg.

Gregg took the paper from under his arm, slapped it against his thigh, and put it back.

The young man smiled and came over to him. "Schwartz?"

"I'm Schwartz. Are you Boris?"

Vasili nodded. This man's voice was not deep, and he did not resemble the picture he had in his mind of Schwartz. He hesitated. Could this be a trap? But why would the American Embassy want to trap him? They wanted to know about Daniels.

"You don't sound like him," Vasili said.

Gregg smiled, glancing at the few figures farther along the walk. "Telephones can be deceiving. Now, what about Lee Daniels?"

Vasili relaxed. "I can tell you where he is being held."

"How would you know that?"

Vasili shrugged. "I have certain friends . . ."

He did not look like a man with high-placed friends. Gregg pursed his lips. But he *did* know about Daniels. And *that* was a secret. The media in the U.S. had mentioned his disappearance several times. *Pravda* had mentioned it once, if he remembered, but then only a brief item. He asked, "What else do you know about Lee Daniels?"

"Isn't it enough I tell you where he is?"

Gregg kept smiling. "Please, don't be annoyed. If I am to give you a large amount of money, I want to be sure of the information. You can understand that."

The mention of a "large amount" was reassuring. "He is a journalist. I have never seen him so I cannot tell you what he looks like."

"He is alive?"

"Yes, certainly. He is being detained by the K.G.B. in a very secret place. It happens my brother works in the complex where he is. From what he has told me, I have put two and two together."

"I see. You are certain it is Daniels?"

Vasili was getting edgy at the questioning. His voice took on a harsher note. "You know Daniels is missing —how many American journalists are missing!?"

"All right . . ."

"Of course it is Daniels."

"And who else have you told?"

Vasili shook his head. "No one at all."

"Not a girl friend or a wife?"

"No. Certainly not. I have kept this as a business deal."

Gregg walked slowly toward the river as they talked. He rubbed his chin as if assessing the information. He nodded his head as they reached the railing above the river. No one was in sight in either direction. Darkness was closing down.

Gregg pulled a silenced automatic and shot Vasili three times in the chest.

Then he pushed the body over into the water.


On the outskirts of Moscow, Loughlin hot-wired a dark blue Toyota four-door sedan.

At a pay telephone Stone called Rima. It was still dark, near dawn, and she was groggy with sleep but woke in a hurry when she realized who was calling. "Mark! Where are you?"

"In Moscow. Meet us by the Metro station close to your apartment . . . How soon can you come?"

"In twenty minutes."

"Good girl." He hung up.

She was as good as her word. When they drove slowly by the station she was there, stamping her feet against the chill. She ran and got into the car as Stone waved, and Loughlin drove on quickly.

"Where have you been!"

"Out of town," Stone told her. "We got into a wild-goose chase and just got back."

She said, "I talked to Davison yesterday and he's worried sick about you. You just dropped out of sight! He was afraid it was another Lee Daniels case."

"Call the embassy then and explain that we're okay. But don't talk to anyone but him."

"Okay."

"Do you know a character named Vasili? He hung out at the Hotel Vilna and sold info to foreign journalists."

She shook her head. Then frowned. "There was

someone by that name found in the river a few days ago." She brightened. "But it's not an uncommon name."

"How did he get in the river?"

"I think the paper said he was shot."

"Ask Davison about him. It sounds suspicious."

"All right. Do you have a place to live?"

"No. That's next on the agenda."

Rima was silent for a moment. "You know the police are looking everywhere for you . . ."

Hog said, "We been dodging the militia and the whole Red Army. We don't care about a few cops."

She gave him a weak smile. "Everyone else does." She patted his cheek. "But I've got an idea. I have a friend who's in Germany at the moment. She'll be there on business for another week at least. I have the key to her apartment because I take care of her plants."

"We can water plants," Loughlin said. "Dainty as anything."

"Well, you could sleep there, but no one must know you're in the apartment. The neighbors would turn you in."

"It's a deal," Stone said, looking around at Hog. "Quiet as a Texas mouse."

"Hell," Hog growled. "I got mice linin' up to take lessons. You look up *quiet* in the book and you going to find a picture of me. Silent Wiley they called me as a kid."

Rima laughed. "I will never believe a word of what you say!"

Hog sounded hurt. "Honey, I invented tippy-toes."

"Where is this place?" Loughlin asked.

"Close to where I live." Rima looked out at the sky.

"But it's too light to go there now. You'll have to wait till dark."

"All right. We'll find a place to—"

"No, come to my apartment. There is a car park by the house, and come in one at a time. You can't sleep on the streets. If you try to sleep in the car, someone is sure to report you."

Hog grinned at her. "And we've got a trunk full of guns."

"Oh, my God! You have?"

"The Russkis keep giving them to us," Hog explained.

"And this man, Vasili, set it all up. He must have been very persuasive."

"He told a pretty good story. Good enough so that we had to check it out."

She sighed. "What are you going to do now?"

"As far as we know, Rybak is still playing poker at the hotel." Stone shrugged. "We'll go back to plan A. Grab him and ask him to talk to us."

"*Ask* him?"

"Certainly," Loughlin said. "I'm sure he'll want to cooperate with us when we show him the right path."


Leonard Schwartz finished his soup in the coffee shop and pushed the empty bowl away, reaching for a pack of cigarettes. He smiled as a skinny man with horn-rimmed glasses came over to the table.

"Sit down, John. How's things?"

John Davison put his tray on the table and pulled out a chair. "Could be worse. How's yourself?"

"I see you're trying the omelet. I guess that's safe."

Davison buttered a roll. "They tell me there's a new cook."

Schwartz blew smoke. "How'd that ever turn out— that matter with Boris?"

Davison hesitated. "Oh yes . . . Boris."

"He offered to sell us info. Said he knew where Daniels was being kept."

"I remember. It was the day I was out sick. Jerry Gregg went to meet him but Boris didn't show."

"Oh yeah? He sounded desperate. Needed money and all that. I'm surprised."

"Gregg's report says he did exactly as you said, stayed there an hour, but no show."

"Huuum. Well, it happens. Too bad."

"Maybe he got picked up."

"Yeah, maybe." Schwartz ground out the cigarette in a tray and got up. "Well, see you later . . ."

Davison watched him go. He thought back. Mark Stone had had reservations about Gregg . . . Was it possible the man was a double agent? Or had he just plain gotten involved somehow with the K.G.B., been entangled and had to supply them—for whatever reason . . .

It happened before and would doubtless happen again.

How would he manage a clandestine check on Gregg that would be definite?


Rima took them to her friend's apartment. It was in another huge apartment block, on the second floor. It was one room, a tiny bath, a cubicle kitchen, and a little balcony crammed with plants.

Unless Rima shouted it in a Metro station there was no way the K.G.B. would find them.

Covering all the windows, with a single candle burning, they discussed grabbing Yuri Rybak and decided to go with their original plan. Loughlin would find a van and park it behind the hotel, and Stone and Hog would do the rest. With any luck it would be a piece of cake.

"After we grab him," Loughlin asked, "then what?"

"We drive somewhere, out of town, anywhere, while we reason with him."

Hog said softly, tapping his chin with a finger, "And after he tells us where Daniels is, then what?"

"We go after Daniels."

Hog persisted. "Rybak. Do we shoot him, take him with us, or what?"

"Tex is right." Loughlin nodded. "We turn him loose and he'll bring the whole bloody Red Army down on our necks."

"We bundle him up somewhere," Stone said, "but that's a bridge we'll cross when we get to it."

Hog remarked to no one in particular, "Rybak's gonna know we can't turn him loose."

Stone shrugged. "If we worry him enough maybe he won't think of that."

Loughlin went out hunting for a van.

He was back in a very short time saying he'd gotten lucky. He had expected to be hunting for hours but only a mile or so away he had watched a man park a well-kept BMW and lock it carefully in a carport.

When the man disappeared, Loughlin appropriated the vehicle.

He left it in a nearby car park. Then, a few hours later, they went out and got in and Loughlin drove to the hotel saying the Germans really knew how to build cars and they ought to steal nothing but German cars in the future. As long as they were in Russia, that is.

It was a bit after nine o'clock when they arrived in the alley and parked the van. Stone got out, smoothed his overcoat, combed his hair, and went up the back stairs and into the poker room as if he belonged there. The room was crowded, a babble of voices; conversations about the races, politics, women, and even Lady Luck. He ordered a beer at the bar and chatted for a moment with the bartender, a young Scotsman who said he was merely substituting for the regular. Yes, he knew who Yuri Rybak was, and thought he was expected.

"They tell me he comes in about this time."

"I think he does, yes. The Russians keep crazy hours."

Stone wandered from one table to the next, watching the play as he finished the beer. Someone came round with a clipboard and papers and asked him if he would sign the Brighton-Ames protest, and Stone said he already had. The man thanked him and moved on.

He had no idea what the protest was.

Heading down the back steps, he joined Hog at the bottom. They took up station in the shadows while Loughlin remained behind the wheel of the van.

But it was another hour before a black Moskvich came speeding down the alleyway and swerved into a parking spot behind the hotel. A man jumped out and opened the rear door.

Yuri Rybak got out.

He was wearing a long black overcoat and no hat. Stone recognized him instantly from the photos.

As Rybak walked toward the rear door, the driver got back in the black car. It was only a few dozen steps to the door and, as Rybak reached it, Hog stepped out and Stone closed in behind the Russian, pushing the .45 in the other's back.

Rybak halted instantly and his face seemed to turn

pale. He said something to them and Hog's huge hands clamped on his shoulders.

The driver got out of the car and another man jumped out on the far side, both whipping out pistols.

Loughlin laid the AK across the door sill of the van and fired a long burst that echoed in the alley. The men were hurled down like rag dolls. Neither got off a shot.

Hog propelled the Russian to the van and tossed him in. Loughlin revved the engine as they piled in, backed, and sped out of the alley. It was all done in seconds.

They had Rybak.

# Chapter Thirteen

Zarnov felt a cold rage. The fact that three foreigners could enter the Soviet Union and make a mockery of every policing, secret, and army organization was outrageous! It had never happened before.

Unmistakably the three Americans were at the bottom of it all, starting with the killing of a K.G.B. man at the Kiev Station.

And now they had killed a dozen or more! They seemed to appear like a whirlwind, destroying and maiming, then disappearing into thin air.

Zarnov had a dozen photographs propped up on his desktop. They had been taken as the Americans entered the Soviet Union in the entourage of Senator Harler. They showed three big, powerful-looking men in ordinary suits, each smiling and innocent of guile, posing for the Russian cameraman. Their luggage had been searched and researched for false bottoms and secret enclosures, and the Customs men had found nothing.

Yet the three had acquired guns and equipment—from the C.I.A.? Or from the American Embassy?

Probably a bit of both. And of course they had acquired Russian equipment from the men they had killed. The list of crimes against them was growing.

But why were they in the Soviet Union in the first place? Zarnov was not an investigator. His inquiries had run into stone walls; investigators were notoriously closemouthed and jealous of their territory. He would be told what he needed to know in due time. Even Pyotr Metkin was difficult. "There could be many reasons why they are here," was all he would say.

Zarnov glowered at the photographs, studying them, feeling frustrated. It had crossed his mind that the three might be trying to free the American journalist, Daniels.

But then, Daniels was well hidden . . .

He sighed. It was not his job to track anyone down. Pyotr Metkin was a man with a long nose and sharp ears, born to sniff and spy. The K.G.B. had none better. He would root out the Americans if anyone could.

Near the end of the day Zarnov received a call from one of his agents and went to meet the man. He chose a photographer's shop for the occasion. It was off Prospekt Mira and the shop had a convenient rear entrance off a long dark alley that went through to another street. When Zarnov appeared, the owner went upstairs to his apartment and left Zarnov alone.

Jerry Gregg was on time and they sat in the darkroom with a tiny red light glowing. Zarnov lit a cigarette. "Why did you come here?"

"Because Davison is suspicious of me."

"What have you done to make him suspicious?"

"I don't know. I think he isn't sure but I feel his eyes on me constantly."

"Do you think you may be overreacting?"

Gregg snapped, "I am positive he suspects me—ever since the affair at the Kiev Station. Someone was in too much of a hurry."

Zarnov thought of Pyotr.

"And when I reported the man, Boris." Gregg shook his head. "That was a mistake."

"I did not order that."

Gregg nodded. "I know. But when I reported to Davison that Boris had not made an appearance—and when a body was found!"

"What are you suggesting?"

"Transfer me. Give me another name and background."

Zarnov puffed the cigarette in silence for a moment. He did not want to lose such a good contact in the American Embassy, but it looked as if events had ended it. Maybe Gregg had been overeager, or Pyotr had.

If Davison could convince his superiors that Gregg was compromised, they would send Gregg home to America. Pack your bags and get out.

Or they might set a trap for him.

It was a dilemma. Lee Daniels had disappeared in the Soviet Union. How would it look to the world if Jerry Gregg also disappeared? If he did what Gregg wanted, he would have to disappear.

He could not take the chance. Let them send Gregg home.

Zarnov put out the cigarette. "You must then avoid traps. Do your work with blinders on, looking neither to right nor left. Will you do that?"

Gregg sighed. "If I must."

"I think you must. They have no real evidence against you?"

"No, I'm certain they do not."

"Very good. Be a model employee. Be perfect. Do you have anything for me?"

"Only a name. I overheard Davison use it and I think he was talking about the three mercenaries."

Zarnov leaned forward. "What was the name?"

"Rima."

"That's all? Just Rima?"

"I know it's a common name—"

"There must be a million Rimas in the Soviet Union!"

Gregg nodded.

"All right. Thank you."

Gregg left the shop first on his bicycle. Zarnov smoked another cigarette and thought about Rima. Undoubtedly the Americans had a number of safe houses in Moscow—his men had them too—and this Rima person could be nothing more than the owner of one.

It was very probable. He had read no report that said a woman was with the three Americans.

When he got back to his office there was a message waiting for him. He swore horribly when he read it.

Yuri Rybak had been kidnapped—probably by those very Americans.


Rybak was terrified when Hog tied his hands behind him and sat him up against the wall of the van. "Take my money!" he gasped in English. "Take the money and let me go."

"We don't want your money," Stone told him.

Hog said, "Shall we cut him first or d'you want to break his legs? The last time we broke somebody's legs he cooperated very fast."

"That's right, he did," Stone agreed.

"Wait, wait!" Rybak yelled. "What is it you want?"

Stone looked surprised. "You want to tell us already?

It's better if we hurt you first. Then your friends won't blame you so much for telling us."

"Tell you what? What is it you want?"

Hog had a length of pipe. He tested it by slapping it into one huge palm. Rybak watched him with round eyes, all the color drained from his face. Hog said, "It's best if we break at least one leg." He pulled one of Rybak's legs out, holding it though the man yelled and tried to yank it back. "What if I just smash the ankle?"

Rybak was yelling and crying at the same time, "No, no, no, I will tell you—what is it you want to know?"

Stone put his hand out. "Don't hit him yet."

"But it won't take a second to smash the ankle—"

"No, wait a minute." Stone looked at Rybak. "You want to tell us?"

"Yes, yes, yes! What is it?"

"Where is Lee Daniels?"

Rybak took a gulp of air, staring at him. "Daniels!?"

"Yes, the American journalist."

Rybak shook his head.

Hog lifted the pipe. He pulled the leg taut and grimaced, about to bring the pipe down.

Rybak screamed. "I will tell you, I will tell you!"

Frowning as if in disappointment, Hog looked at Stone, who said, "Very well . . ."

Rybak was sweating. He looked like a man who had just run forty miles in a blizzard. He was panting and trembling—he *believed* the huge man who still held his foot.

"Go on," Stone urged.

"He is held in the mental hospital at Chelkar." Rybak closed his eyes and sagged like a bundle of old rags.

Hog said, "Can we believe him?"

Tears were streaming down Rybak's face and he was shaking with fear. Stone nodded. Rybak didn't dare lie.

• • •

They tied the man up and put a blanket over him. Spreading out the map, they located Chelkar. It was at the edge of the city. Stone said, "Let's take a look at it." He climbed up front with Loughlin.

The hospital was set back from the road with old trees around it. The main building looked very old, as if it had once been a mansion. They saw no guards as they drove past.

"There will be guards," Loughlin said, "if Daniels is in there."

"Let's park it and take a closer look. There's other buildings behind the big one. What time is it?"

"Plenty of time till sunrise." Loughlin slowed the van and made a U turn. As they approached the hospital again he pulled into a side road and halted the van under some spreading trees.

Stone made a sign to Hog and got out, closing the door silently. There was no one in sight in any direction. He crossed the road and halted under a tree, looking everywhere. He moved to the next tree. A cold ground mist shortened the distances and made a halo around a light far off to his right.

Close up, he saw the building was of stone, gray in the meager light, and four stories tall. Several small lights burned inside, and all the windows on the first two floors were barred.

He came to a small wrought-iron fence, more decorative than protective. He slid over it and approached the end of the main building.

A guard came trudging around the corner and Stone flattened himself on the dewy grass. The man walked by no more than ten feet away without noticing him. Now and then he flicked a flashlight back and forth at random.

Stone got up and went around the corner. There was a high, formidable hedge and beyond it a large grassy area. To the right were two more long wooden buildings that looked for all the world like U.S. Army hospital wards. Smoke was rising from one end of the nearest. Possibly the guard shack.

There was a single truck and two small cars far along by the third building, and as he watched a man came out of the ward where the smoke was rising, and walked toward him.

Stone faded back and went through the hedge to the front.

Crossing the road again, he got into the van. "It's not very big, three buildings. I think Daniels must be in the stone one. The others look pretty flimsy."

"Guards?" Loughlin asked.

"I saw two. They probably keep circling the lot. But this isn't a high-security prison, so guards are probably minimal. Secrecy is the thing."

"We could use a plan of the place," Hog offered.

Stone nodded. "I wonder if Senator Harler could get one for us? He's got ways and means."

"We'll try him." Loughlin turned the key and the engine caught. They drove back into the town.

It began to rain lightly as they approached the apartment. Hog bundled Rybak in the blanket and carried him into the house as he might an ordinary package. They left him the blanket but took his pants and shoes, just in case.

When it got light, Stone hunted up a pay telephone and called the embassy, asking for Senator Harler. The senator was unavailable; he settled for Davison, telling him what they needed.

Davison said, "Daniels is at the mental hospital at Chelkar?"

"Yes, do you know it?"

"I've been there. We had a nurse go nuts last year. Thought she was a jar of applesauce. Weird case."

"Can you draw us a plan?"

"Let me work on it. How do you know he's there?"

"We reasoned with a government official."

Davison hesitated. "I guess I'd better not ask anything more, huh?"

"Maybe not. When shall I call you again?"

"Give me three or four hours."

"Okay." Stone hung up, glancing at his watch.

Zarnov settled himself in his big office chair and frowned at the opposite wall. Rybak kidnapped? Why would anyone kidnap *him?*

He had received a written report and he read it again. There were no eyewitnesses. Several men had run out on hearing the shots, but they had seen no one alive. Rybak's two bodyguards were dead, torn to pieces by AK rounds. They had not fired a shot.

It sounded like the three Americans all right. But why had they kidnapped Rybak instead of killing him with the others?

Zarnov folded the report and unfolded it, smoothing it out. Rybak's job was to oversee the foreign correspondents, men who were seldom impressed by the Soviet Union's laws. Russian authorities considered them troublemakers and restricted them whenever it was possible —without causing international flaps. There had been much trouble in the past. A number of journalists had had to be deported because they ignored Russian regulations. Rybak had been instrumental in those deportations.

And now Lee Daniels had disappeared. The U.S. had made a stink about it. All the foreign journalists were seething. It could happen to any one of them, they said publicly. .

Many blamed Rybak for the disappearance. So perhaps someone was revenging himself on Rybak.

Zarnov shook out a pack of cigarettes, selected one, and lit it. It was the most likely explanation, wasn't it?

Except that it didn't *feel* right to him.

Would someone set a trap for Rybak, knowing he had bodyguards and knowing he'd have to kill those bodyguards to get to Rybak? Was revenge that dear to someone? And if this mysterious someone was willing to murder two men to get at Rybak, why not just kill Rybak, too? Did he want to take the man somewhere and torture him?

Zarnov shook his head. It just did not feel right. He ought to talk to Pyotr Metkin about it.

What the hell was Rybak doing in that particular place anyway . . . in an alley behind a hotel?

He looked at the report again. It did not mention *why* Rybak had been found there. Well, maybe the man had a woman in the hotel. *That* was likely.

Reaching for the telephone, he had himself put through to Pyotr Metkin. "In the matter of Rybak, the man who was kidnapped last night . . ."

"Hello, Colonel. Why are you interested in Rybak?"

"Because the three Americans may have captured him."

"Why do you think that?"

"Because of the way it was done."

Metkin was silent a moment.

"Pyotr?"

"Yes, I see what you mean. We had thought it might have been a simple robbery."

Zarnov shook his head. "I think it may have been more than that."

"Of course you're guessing . . ."

"Have you been to the site? Why was Rybak in an alley behind the hotel?"

Metkin chuckled. "He was in the habit of gambling with the foreign press."

"Gambling!" Zarnov was astonished.

"You didn't know he was a gambler? He loved to play poker with the American reporters. They tell me he learned the game when he was stationed in New York."

Zarnov frowned. "Then he could have been robbed —if they played for high stakes."

"Yes, but why would a robber kidnap him?" Metkin cleared his throat. "First we thought it might have been robbery, but now I doubt it very much. But I hadn't thought of the American mercenaries. What would they want with Rybak?"

"I don't know . . ."

"If you think of anything, please let me know." Metkin hung up.

So Rybak had been a gambler . . . with the foreign press, and especially with American reporters. Doubtless he practiced his English on them.

But everyone knew how violent Americans could be. Look at their movies!

He lit another cigarette and stared out of the window. What did Rybak know that the Americans would want? Did Rybak know where Daniels was being held?

Zarnov wanted answers. And he was prepared to do *anything* to get them.

# Chapter Fourteen

Davison stepped out of a taxi on Gorky Street and began to walk northwest. In the second block he was joined by Mark Stone, who came from a doorway. He passed over a slip of paper, which Stone pocketed.

"It's as good a plan as I could do," Davison said. "Three of us worked on it. Of course they might have changed the rooms in the last few months . . ."

"What about guards?"

"The ones I saw were all retired types, maybe ex-police or army. It's not a high-risk place, you know."

"Okay. Anything else?"

"Senator Harler wants to make a big stink about it, send an international commission to the hospital—"

Stone shook his head. "At the first sign of it they'd move Daniels fast and they'd find nothing."

"That's what I told him."

"Is he convinced?"

"I don't think so, but he's agreed to keep his mouth shut until you do your job."

"Good."

"That's it?"

At Stone's nod, Davison turned toward the street and raised his arm, signaling for a taxi. Stone paused in the first doorway, watching the street.

No one was watching him.

He walked two blocks, then took a taxi back to a row of shops near the apartment, giving the driver instructions in halting German. A great many people spoke German, Rima had said.

On a table they smoothed out Davison's plan of the hospital floors. They looked very much like floor plans of an ordinary hospital. There were several dozen rooms. Daniels might be in any one of them.

Loughlin said, "But they've certainly put him by himself, and not in an ordinary ward."

Stone nodded. "Maybe he's not in this building at all." He frowned toward the abject Rybak. "Let's discuss this with our Russian friend."

Hog brought the man to the table and they showed him the plans. Rybak asked, "What is this?"

"Floor plans of the asylum. Where is Daniels being held?"

"I don't know."

Hog tapped him. "Be very careful with the truth."

Rybak shrank away from him. "How would I know? I have never been in that place. I know only that he is there."

Stone studied the man. Rybak certainly looked like a weasel who had served a long term for some monstrous crime. From that face everything would sound like a lie.

Hog said casually, "Why don't you all go out and leave me with him for a while."

"No, no, no! He will kill me!" Rybak was terrified of the big Texan. "Don't go, don't go!" He grabbed at Stone's arm.

Stone freed himself. "What else can you tell us about this hospital?"

Rybak wailed, "I have never been there! I know nothing about it! Please, I am telling the truth! I know nothing about it."

Stone looked at the others and Loughlin nodded; Hog shrugged. He probably was telling the truth.


It was an hour after midnight when the van halted under the trees across from the asylum. Stone led the way through the trees, past the hedge to a point at the side of the main stone building where they could see the guard shack. Smoke was rising from it as before.

Two guards were standing in front of the long wooden building, talking in low tones. They watched as one went inside and the other came toward them. He was middle-aged, carrying an AK-47 slung over his shoulder and a flashlight in his hand. As he reached them, Hog tripped him, Stone grabbed his hands, and Loughlin put a gag into his mouth.

He was trussed up in moments and carried to a spot under a row of shrubs.

Loughlin took the flashlight and the AK. Stone investigated the rear door of the building. It was very large with ornate sculpting; the door itself was of heavy wood and had an impressive brass lock.

Stone stripped off a length of moulding to get at the lock with his knife. Using both hands with the blade, he cut away the wood around the lock. It wasn't neat, but effective. In a few minutes he had the door open.

Hog stepped through, his pistol ready. There was a wide corridor running from front to back and narrower halls to right and left. There was only one small light burning near the door and the floor was silent. Close to the door was a chair and table with a small lamp. Stone felt the lamp bulb. It was cold.

They moved along the corridor looking into rooms. None of the doors was locked. There was no one in any of the rooms. At the end, Loughlin whispered, "The place is empty, mates."

"Maybe he's upstairs."

Hog moved toward a door that had a legend written on it in Russian. He opened the door and looked at a stairway down. There was a light on in the basement. He pointed.

As if he had touched a switch, a loud bell on the outside of the building began to ring. Loughlin said, "What the bloody hell!"

"We tripped a silent alarm," Stone snapped. "Get out —let's hop it!"

Men yelled outside and they heard an automobile drive up, tires screeching.

"They don't know it's us," Stone said. He ran to the front door but someone was there, on the other side. "Damn."

"They're at the back," Hog remarked. He leveled his AK and sent a burst down the corridor. Someone screamed and the doorway was clear.

"Try the windows." Stone ran along a narrow hallway. All the windows were barred. Sonofabitch, he had noted that the first day.

The alarm bell was still ringing, now a monotonous

sound. How many had they to contend with? Just those overage guards? Could there be more than a half dozen of them?

Of course they would have called for help . . .

Stone ran back to the front door. On one knee he aimed at the door lock and fired the AK. The heavy bullets smashed a hole the size of his head.

A whistle sounded outside and someone yelled. Hog slid along the doorjamb and his pistol cracked once, twice, three times; then he beckoned. He pushed the door open wide. Loughlin slid through, looking for a target.

A bullet hit the door just above his head and Stone turned, flopping on his stomach, cradling the AK. Several shadows were slipping through the rear door. He fired a burst, then another, and it was quiet.

Then Loughlin yelled.

Scrambling up, Stone ran out into the dark and halted under the trees. Hog and Loughlin had one of the guards on the grass, tieing him with his own belt.

Hog said, "Thought we'd reason with this turkey. I think he speaks English." He picked the man up and they hurried toward the road.

Crossing the road, Hog tossed the prisoner in the back of the van and Loughlin fired it up . . . then cut the engine. "Listen."

Trucks were roaring along the road. Craning his neck, Stone watched two personnel carriers turn into the asylum with screeching wheels. Their headlights disappeared and he nudged the Briton.

"Get this mother moving."

Loughlin tooled the van onto the road without lights and they headed toward the city. No one followed them. After a mile he switched on the lights.

In the back of the van Hog sat the guard up and asked him his name.

"Anton."

"You do speak English."

"A little." He was a chubby, sparse-haired man of about fifty, obviously frightened.

Stone climbed into the rear. "Where is the American journalist?"

The man bit his lip. "I am only gaurd."

"Hand me that iron," Hog said. "Did you wipe the blood off it?" He smiled at Anton. "We smashed a feller's ankle yesterday when he didn't figger to talk."

Stone handed him the tire iron. He pushed Anton's chest as Hog grabbed the man's leg and straightened it.

Anton yelped, "What you do!?"

The big Texan touched Anton's ankle bone with the heavy iron. Leaning in close, he scowled. "You talk, comrade, huh? You talk or I break your foot."

Stone asked pleasantly, "Where is the American journalist being held?"

Anton was sweating. He ignored Stone, all his attention focused on Hog, staring as if he wondered if the man were insane. He pulled ineffectually at his leg.

Stone tapped the man's chest. "Where is the American journalist?"

Hog tapped the ankle hard. Anton jumped and screamed. He yelled, "I am only guard!"

Hog made a savage face and lifted the tire iron as if about to bring it down. He flattened Anton's foot with the other hand.

Anton shouted, "I tell you! I tell you!"

Hog smiled. He put down the iron. "Well, that's better, little friend." He patted Anton's cheek.

The Russian collapsed. He had gone white. He was breathing hard, eyes closed. He opened them slowly as Hog pulled him up by the shirtfront.

"Where is he?"

"Leningrad! They take him Leningrad!"

"How do you know?"

"Driver tell me. He live there. We smoke cigarette, talk."

Stone nodded. "Okay. Where in Leningrad?"

"Hospital!"

Loughlin said, "That's where they keep drugs."

Stone asked, "Which hospital?"

Anton shrugged. "It say Paschenko on truck."

"Paschenko is a hospital?"

"*Da*. Big place." Anton nodded vigorously.

"Stop the van," Stone called.

Loughlin glanced around and pulled over.

Stone said, "Let him go." He tapped Anton's chest. "If you tell them you were captured by us and told us where the American was taken, what would they do? Do you understand the question?"

Anton nodded quickly, his shoulders slumped. "They put me prison. Never get out."

"Maybe shoot you." Hog offered.

"Yes, maybe."

"Or Siberia."

Anton sighed deeply.

Hog patted the man's cheek again. "Then, comrade, do not tell them."

"Good advice," Stone said. "Do not tell them."

"I think, good advice." Color began to come back into Anton's cheeks. "Not tell them."

"Let him out," Stone said. "He's got religion."

•   •   •

An hour later, Stone talked to Davison on a pay-phone. "Daniels has been moved. We have reason to believe it's to Leningrad."

"Leningrad!"

"Yes. Do you know a place called the Paschenko Hospital?"

"No. Never heard of it."

"Can you find out?"

"Yeah. Lemme see what I can do. Give me a few hours."

"Right."

# Chapter Fifteen

They had given him a tray of food the third day and he wolfed it down, trembling and very shaky. Daniels had never had to diet in his life and was not accustomed to missing meals. His captors could easily "forget" to feed him and he would die in this iron box.

It seemed to him that the nights were getting colder also, but maybe it was because he felt weaker. He often sat on the bunk with a blanket around his shoulders, putting himself back in the States, in familiar surroundings with loved ones. Did anyone know he was here? Did anyone care? It was too easy to believe he was alone, and when he sank into that morass he had to jerk himself up and out of it. Surely someone was asking questions about him . . .

Zarnov did not come again with his demands.

But three guards appeared while he was sleeping. The heavy door clanged open and they pulled him off the bunk, threw his clothes on him, and indicated he should get dressed.

None of them spoke English.

Daniels shoved his few possessions into his pockets and was hustled along the corridor, through barred doors and upstairs and out into the night. He had a quick glimpse of the gray stone building, barred on the first two floors, and caught sight of the two long wooden structures near it before they shoved him into a van and slammed the door.

He was knocked off his feet as the car surged forward, and he clawed his way to a bench to hold on.

The van did not stop again for more than two hours. They let him out for a moment to urinate, then shoved him back in again and went on. It seemed to get even colder and rain began to patter on the roof.

Where the hell were they taking him?

He managed to wedge himself into a corner and, though the road was filled with potholes, he could doze for periods, until they woke him by violent bumping. Didn't they fix their roads in Russia?

Once they stopped for a long time, an hour or more, and he managed to sleep. But woke when the van began to jolt and sway again.

The rain got very heavy for a time and the van slowed, creeping along, and he could hear water splashing. They rumbled over bridges and once in a while met other trucks or vehicles. Daniels could hear them coming, passing and departing.

Finally it began to get light. After a while he could make out the end of the van, then his surroundings... not much to see.

Where the hell were they taking him?

Russia was generally one huge flat plain; apparently

the mountains had been ground down by glacier action thousands of years ago. They'd traversed very few hills and they had been driving for hours . . . and it had gradually been getting colder. Were they taking him into the Arctic?

But then the road began to get better, and finally they were on paved streets. They were in a city. He could hear traffic and feel that people and buildings were around them.

Could it be Leningrad?

Leningrad was a hell of a long way off, something like eight hundred miles, Davison said. And yes, there was a Paschenko Hospital in the suburbs. "How are you going to get there?"

"In a car, I suppose."

"Let me meet you with a suggestion. Same place as last time. Okay? In an hour."

"Right," Stone said.

He was in the doorway watching as Davison got out of the taxi and began walking.

When he joined the other, Davison said, "There's an underground in Russia, you know. The government denies it, of course, but we work with it now and then, supply them with money at times and with forged materials. We scratch each other's backs."

"Good," Stone said. "I like the sound of it."

"I think we can get you to Leningrad so nobody knows it. The train would be faster but also more dangerous. Your photos have been circulated. Every militiaman and every K.G.B. man has them tattooed on his eyeballs. Depend on it."

"You have a name for us?"

Davis handed him a slip of paper. "It's all on this. He

expects your call—give him the code word, Geronimo."

"Okay." Stone glanced at the paper. "I hope he speaks English."

"Yes. Matter of fact he lived for a long time in Cincinnati, where he taught school."

"He's American?"

"Well, he was born in a little town near the Black Sea but he speaks English as well as any of us. That phone number will be good for another four hours." Davison looked at his watch. "Yes, about four hours. Then he'll leave."

"Careful."

"Yes, has to be. Well, I think that's all. He will fill you in."

"Okay. Thanks."

Davison nodded and halted at the curb to wave for a taxi.

Stone walked on, around the next corner and paused in a doorway. The name was Kyril Andronov. Under it was a number, and under that two words: *Burn this*.

In a public building he found a pay telephone. A man answered at once and Stone said, "Geronimo."

"No names," the voice said. "I will give you directions."

"Okay."

"Begin with the Simonov Station of the Prospekt Mira Metro north. You know where it is?"

"Yes. About a mile from here."

"Good. Now, a football team minus three. Take the number of possible Series games from that."

"Got it."

"The remainder is the number past Simonov where I will meet you in less than an hour. Can you do that?"

"Yes."

"All right. I will be outside on the street and I will carry a book in my hand." He hung up.

Stone smiled. That meant the first station past Simonov. Stone hurried to the car where Loughlin waited. Hog was in the apartment with Rybak.

"Back to get Hog," he said, and told Loughlin what Andronov and Davison had said.

"Very cagey," Loughlin commented. "How many Series games *are* possible? I suppose you mean World Series."

"Seven."

"Oh. I would have said five."

"Well, you don't know your ass about baseball."

Loughlin grinned. "True. Let's hope the Russkis don't either."

They drove back to the apartment and Hog carried the bundle to the van and put it in the back. He had Rybak tied and gagged and wrapped in a blanket.

"He's been very good," Hog said, unwrapping the blanket so Rybak could breathe. "I told him if he made no trouble we wouldn't cut his throat till maybe later tonight."

"Nothing but heart," Loughlin remarked.

Hog was astonished to hear there was a Russian underground. "I thought they had everyone cataloged. The Russkis are slipping up. They must be just as fucked up as everybody."

"Yeah, when they've got big shots like him." Loughlin jerked his thumb toward Rybak.

It was a long drive across town and Loughlin was extremely careful. It wouldn't do to have a policeman stop them. There seemed to be nothing but trucks and taxis on the streets. He turned left on Mira and drove for a mile before pulling over.

"Here it is, the stop after Simonov. Where's your guy?"

"We could be early—no, there's a citizen with a book." A poorly dressed tall man came to the curb carrying a red book in his hand. He was watching the traffic.

They paused by him and Stone said, "Geronimo."

The man jumped into the van and Loughlin gunned it. Andronov said, "Hello, I'm Andronov. Take the next left."

Stone introduced them quickly. "Where are we going?"

"A couple of miles there's a fenced yard. It's an old pumping station. We'll be safe there. Did you steal this van?"

"Borrowed it," Loughlin told him. "Don't scratch the paint."

Andronov chuckled. He was skinny, with black hair and bright black eyes. He tossed the book in the back and noticed Rybak. "Who's that?"

"He's a Russian official who's been cooperating with us so we don't cut his balls off."

"All right. I won't ask you any more about that. They didn't tell me what you're after—so don't tell me."

"Okay."

"Take a right at the next corner. Go about a half mile."

It was a crummy neighborhood, run-down and decaying. The street was full of potholes and Loughlin had to go very slowly. He glanced at Andronov. "How'd you know about the Series?"

"I played minor league ball for two years." Andronov shrugged. "Couldn't make the majors. I had a good glove but I never could hit a curve ball for sour shit." He gestured. "See that ratty-looking blue building up ahead? Turn in there."

Loughlin slowed to make the turn and the gate opened as if by magic. Andronov said, "Park it anywhere."

The gate closed behind them.

Loughlin turned parallel to the blue building and cut the engine. They were in a cluttered yard with a high board fence. A dark green Moskvich waited near the gate; along one side boxes, crates, and barrels were piled, ready for hauling.

As they got out of the van, Stone saw the man who had let them in, a squat man in overalls and wool cap with a submachine gun on a strap over his shoulder. He was apparently a lookout.

Andronov said, "In here." He led them down some steps to a lower level where it was much colder. They followed in single file, with Hog pushing Rybak along.

A gray corridor, dusty and dank, led to a wooden ladder nailed to the wall. Andronov climbed up it and they followed to find themselves in a large room that had no windows at all. Around the walls were half a dozen iron cots with blankets neatly stacked on each. There were chairs and tables, one set up with chessmen, and several candles and lamps. A single small lamp was burning on one of the tables.

Andronov beckoned Hog and opened a door. "Put him in here."

Hog led Rybak into the small room. It had a cot and nothing else. Rybak flopped on the bed and Andronov closed the door.

"What are you going to do with him?"

Stone said, "We have to hold him for a while. He knows us and knows too much about us."

"I see. Davison tells me you are going to Leningrad."

"Yes. As soon as possible."

"All right. We can get you there. We've got a tractor trailer going there tonight. The rig isn't ours, but the driver is one of us."

Loughlin glanced at the cots. "Are some others coming?"

"No," Andronov replied. "You've seen two of us and you know what we are. We won't question you, and you don't question us. That way we stay alive a little longer. What you don't know you can't tell."

Stone nodded. "You got it."

"Your transportation will be ready about midnight, maybe a little sooner. So in the meantime please stay in this room. Are you going to take the official with you?"

"We'd rather not."

Andronov scratched his chin. "We move around a lot. Have to, you know. The K.G.B. is dumb as hell about some things and smart about others. You never know. We can probably ship him to Siberia for you . . ."

"We'd appreciate it," Stone said. "If anyone deserves Siberia, he does."

"Freeze his ass off," Hog put in.

Andronov nodded. "Wilco. There's food and tea if you want it. Shall we get rid of your van?"

"By all means. Park it somewhere and leave it. It's probably hot as Joe Stalin in hell."

"Nothing's that hot." Andronov gave them a thumbs-up gesture and went down the ladder.

. . .

In full uniform with medals, Colonel Zarnov requested a meeting through channels and met Senator Harler in the Blue Room of the embassy. Zarnov was polite and charming.

They were served coffee and tea and little round raisin cakes, and there was vodka if the colonel preferred.

The conversation was also polite and charming, up to a point.

Zarnov turned it to basics. "We know the names of the three men who came into the Soviet Union as your security persons, Senator."

"The names were on their passports."

"Yes." Zarnov did not for a moment believe the names were real. "If I may ask, Senator, why did you bring them here?"

"As security personnel." Harler smiled winningly.

"But they have not acted as such."

"Ahhh. Your wonderful surveillance! You do keep tabs on us, don't you, Colonel."

Zarnov returned the smile. "I fear their actions have made it impossible for us not to notice them. They killed one of my men in Kiev Station Square, for instance."

"Ahh, I see. You have an eyewitness?"

"Unfortunately no, but—"

"I realize our systems of justice are widely divergent, Colonel, but it really is not enough merely to accuse. *We* require proof. Will you have more tea?"

"Thank you, no." Zarnov motioned with his hand. "Let us not debate the point. But my superiors require an answer of me. It is an important question, Senator. I ask you again . . . why are they here?"

"Because I felt the need of security. You mention a

murder in Kiev Station Square, so close to us here. You see, the streets *are* dangerous."

Zarnov gritted his teeth.

Harler continued, "Perhaps I was wrong about security, but then, I have that choice." He smiled. "You would have that same choice in my country."

Zarnov sighed inwardly. He knew when he was getting nowhere. He fell back on charming, ate a raisin cake, and got out as quickly as he decently could. He had learned nothing.

When he returned to his office there was a note waiting. It was from Pyotr Metkin. Yuri Rybak, the note said, was still missing and feared dead.

There had also been a daring raid, by persons unknown, on the asylum at Chelkar where the American, Lee Daniels, had been held. Unfortunately several were dead, none of them the raiders.

Daniels had been moved to Leningrad the day before. He, Pyotr, had been edgy about Chelkar and his hunch had apparently paid off.

Zarnov rubbed his chin. Yes, the three Americans *are* after Daniels . . .

# Chapter Sixteen

Shortly before midnight, as Andronov had said, it was time. He came for them and led them down to the small Moskvich and they drove farther into the outskirts of the city to stop along a lonely road in the dark.

"The rig will be here soon," Andronov promised. "This is a parallel road to the main highway to Leningrad."

His word was good. In half an hour there were headlights behind them and the big tractor-trailer loomed up out of the night and halted just beyond the little car. The driver got down and Andronov spoke to him a moment, then introduced the three, saying, this is Alexi. He will take you into Leningrad."

Alexi was a short, slender man with a good smile in a rather bland face. "I have just the place for you," he told Andronov, who translated.

There was a cubicle space in the trailer, like the false bottom of a satchel. Probably the underground hauled many things in such spaces. They crowded into it but Alexi left the panel open, telling them through Andronov that they must pull it closed and remain silent if the rig should stop at any time.

"We understand," Stone told him.

Alexi showed them the two metal catches used to unlock the panel from the inside. It was a good, heavy padded panel. There were ventilation holes in the top, which could not be seen from the outside unless one were atop the trailer. And there was a small electric bulb inside the cubicle, which gave plenty of light to see by.

"Not quite as good as jail," Loughlin said.

"It ain't a pigsty," Hog remarked. "It's warm."

"And safe," said Stone.

They bade Andronov good-bye, with thanks, and crawled into the space, and the rig moved out.

It took another lifetime to roll to Leningrad. The rig stopped three times, and each time they locked the panel in place and sat silent in the dark, listening to the mutter of voices somewhere inside. Once questing hands came poking into the trailer but discovered nothing.

When they began to move again, they unlocked the panel and turned on the light.

Their C.I.A contact in Leningrad was a man named Byron Campbell, a veteran of the Russian beat. Stone had a telephone number provided by Davison. When Alexi let them off in the city, Stone called the number and Campbell came to collect them at once.

He had a brown Volga and picked them off the street while it was still dark and drove them by a roundabout route to a safe house in the suburbs.

It was an apartment in one of the ubiquitous slab-sided multiple dwellings that uglify Russia. Campbell

took them to a basement apartment, side by side with
the caretaker's, who was in the pay, Campbell told
them, of the C.I.A. The caretaker, named John Kosova,
lived by himself in one room.

When they were inside with the door locked, Campbell said, "Davison tells me you're after Lee Daniels."

"Yes. We think he's at the Paschenko Hospital. Do
you know it?"

"No. Never been there. But it's a big place, sprawling."

"How can we manage it?"

Campbell shook his head. "You can't. You'd never
get in the gate, any of you. Visitors have to fill out
forms, all the usual Russian rigamarole. Forget it."

Hog asked, "What if we just slide over the fence?"

"Okay. What then? There must be ten or eleven different buildings. Three large ones and lots of small
wards." Campbell smiled ruefully. "It's just not possible."

"Something *has* to be possible," Stone said. "We've
had impossible situations before and they always work
out."

"This is Russia. It's impossible to begin with."
Campbell fiddled with a pipe, chewing the stem. "Let
me see what my boys can find out for you. I've got
some Russian-speaking agents who could con Lenin out
of his *shapka*." He went to the door. "I'll get back to
you. Stay under cover..." He went out.


Colonel Zarnov requested every report that
seemed to have a bearing on the three American commandos. When they came he studied them, looking for
similarities, a handle, anything to lead him to them. But
there was nothing.

The reports were vague, except they enumerated killings laid to the foreigners' door. The three had been involved in several pursuits and had escaped each time. The pursuers had presented annoyingly similar reasons —the Americans had been lucky. He crumpled and hurled the reports across the room. Lucky!

But now Daniels was in Leningrad. It was very unlikely the mercenaries would learn that. Even if they had Yuri Rybak, the man did not know.

He, Zarnov, could relax a bit. Except for his superiors, who were demanding information from Daniels.

He had himself driven to the hospital and was taken to the office of Dr. Ilya Lyudin. Lyudin was a thin balding man with black hair around his ears and neck, a drooping mustache, and huge black eyes behind horn-rimmed glasses. Zarnov thought he looked like a great bug in a long white coat.

The man, Daniels, was being held in a selected ward, Lyudin told him. It had been a prison ward and had barred windows and special nurses and guards. "I am told he is an enemy of the state?"

"Yes, precisely. What is his condition now?"

"He is awake." Lyudin shrugged. "He is normal."

"I wish to have a conversation with him. I wish in fact for him to tell me things he is keeping hidden. Have you a drug for this?"

"Yes, certainly, Colonel. There are a number of drugs. How soon do you—"

"Immediately."

"You mean today?"

"Yes, now. Can you arrange it?"

The doctor nodded. He sat behind his desk and picked up the telephone.

• • •

Byron Campbell was back in the basement apartment an hour after dark. "We have doubts that your man is in Paschenko. My agents can get no smell of him. How sure are you that he's there?"

"We had it from a guard at his last prison."

"He may not have known."

Stone scratched his jaw. "He convinced us."

"Well then, maybe he's been moved. I mean he could have been taken to Paschenko, then moved again."

Loughlin said, "Maybe he's held in tight security."

"That's possible, of course." Campbell sighed. "My guys are very damned sneaky, but there are places in Paschenko they can't get to."

Stone asked, "Can they keep trying?"

"Oh yes. But I do have something else. Does the name Colonel Zarnov mean anything to you?"

"Zarnov . . . ?" Stone glanced at the others, who shook their heads. He said the name again. "Zarnov—I seem to remember Senator Harler mentioning the name . . . I wish I could be sure."

"Well, he's suddenly here in Leningrad."

"Why is it important?"

"Because Zarnov is a K.G.B. hairball. He is just the guy to handle a situation like grabbing Daniels. He has done slime jobs before to our certain knowledge."

"Yes . . . ?"

"Zarnov and his bunch are used to trouble-shooting the K.G.B.'s dirty little deals." Campbell made a face. "Usually he hangs around Moscow, chasing women, and when he shows up here in Leningrad I am suspicious as hell—especially when Lee Daniels has been brought here. I am damn sure there's a connection."

"It could be something else?"

"My guys have their ears to the ground. They don't smell anything as big as Daniels."

"Well, get through to Senator Harler and ask him what he knows. Can do?"

"I'll do it tonight." Campbell went to the door. "You stay outa sight. I'll see you later."

He was back in two hours.

"Yes, Harler knows 'im. The embassy thinks he's a grade-A nerd. Zarnov went to see Harler to ask him about you three, all very diplomatic and sugary. Harler told him zilch."

"We're famous," Hog said.

"In K.G.B. circles," Loughlin remarked.

"Harler thinks Zarnov is in charge of hiding Daniels. He has no doubts about it. He has certain sources."

"Yes, he does. Deep pockets. Rubles talk in the Soviet Union. What do you suggest?"

Campbell smiled. "We have a file on K.G.B. shitheads. Zarnov chases blondes and loves nightclubs. One of these days we may be able to use that. He's also got a dacha up in the woods where he takes women."

Hog asked, "What's a dacha?"

"A pussy place," Loughlin said. "A twatitorium."

"Man!" Campbell said. "You got college men here. I ought to be more respectful."

"Well, you don't have to be a farmer," Stone said seriously, "to be outstanding in your field."

Campbell laughed. "Can we get back tc Zarnov?"

Loughlin grinned. "Maybe we can grab him and give him some of Hog's tire-iron treatment. It works every time."

Stone asked, "Does Zarnov travel with bodyguards?"

"I don't know, but maybe." Campbell shrugged. "I'm sure he thinks himself safe in Leningrad. Not many know him here—so not many enemies. Leningrad is a much friendlier city than Moscow, you know. Do you think he has any idea you three are here?"

"We hope not," Stone said.

Hog grinned. "We love surprising folks."

Stone asked, "Where's a good place to look for him? Where does he live?"

"No chance there. But there's a great place to meet women. It's famous in town, so I'm sure Zarnov would hear about it."

"A nightclub?"

"It's called the Café Dvor. And by the way, I expect to have some photos of Zarnov in the morning. My lads will take them and I'll get copies to you as fast as I can."

"Good show," Loughlin said.

# Chapter Seventeen

Dr. Lyudin stood back from the bed as the two husky attendants took hold of Daniels's arms and held him immobile. Colonel Zarnov, arms crossed over his chest, watched from the doorway.

Deftly then, Lyudin inserted the tube and taped it to the back of Daniels's hand. "Hold him there . . . don't move . . ."

Lyudin adjusted the drops and watched the patient. In a few moments Daniels's eyes drooped and he began to relax. In five minutes the doctor motioned the attendants away. "He will be all right now. You can go."

The attendants left the room, closing the door.

Zarnov asked, "What did you give him?"

"An experimental drug. In a few minutes he will—" Dr. Lyudin paused, frowning. He stepped toward the bed as Daniels suddenly jerked, his head turned, and he vomited over the bed and floor!

Instantly Zarnov ran to the door yelling for the attendants.

Lyudin was swearing. He grabbed Daniels's arm and managed to rip off the tape, holding the wound with his thumb. Daniels was retching and jerking, pale as paper and gasping.

The attendants ran in and Lyudin gave them instructions as Zarnov stepped into the corridor. Obviously the drug had affected Daniels adversely. He swore under his breath. This would slow up the process.

Everyone was different. Lyudin kept a careful history, writing in a small, neat hand—unusual for a physician—in a leather-bound notebook. He had seen this same rejection once before, though not as violent. He had had Daniels's heart monitored and was gratified that the heartbeat had gradually become normal after a number of hours.

When Colonel Zarnov called, requesting he use another drug on the patient, Lyudin had asked him calmly if he had any interest in Daniels's life. "If the man dies in my care, may I list your name on my report?"

Zarnov hung up on him.

Dr. Lyudin spoke aloud to the empty room, expressing his opinion of the K.G.B. in general, and Zarnov in particular. This off his chest, he went on with his work.

Campbell appeared with an envelope containing half a dozen candid shots of Colonel Zarnov. They had all been taken at a distance with a telephoto lens but showed Zarnov very clearly from several angles.

Stone propped them up and they studied them closely while Campbell explained that the Café Dvor was on the corner of Nevsky Prospekt, across the river.

"You will find West Europeans there, some Finns,

and many girls who are parading their wares."

Hog said, "Hookers in Russia?"

"You bet. And guys like Zarnov run after them." Campbell struck a match and held it over his pipe, blowing smoke. "I can't tell you much else. He hasn't been here long enough for my lads to check him out thoroughly."

"Anything more from Paschenko Hospital?"

"Well, yes, a smell. As I told you, there is a prison ward there that's not used much. But one of my boys thinks it may be in use now." He accented, *"May* be. It's under surveillance at this moment."

"What's the best time to go to the café?" Stone asked.

"Late. Ten or eleven I'd say. The early crowd is gone by then and the real drinkers come in."

"Time is running out for Lee Daniels, and for us," Stone grunted. "It might be time to stack this deck if we can."

"You mean, try and get Zarnov out of that club to us, instead of going in after him like we tried with Rybak," Loughlin thought aloud.

"Any chance of sending in a ringer?" Stone asked. "Have you been able to learn just what kind of ladies our boy Zarnov goes for?"

"Ladies," Hog snorted. "We are talking pros here, ain't we? Not that I got anything against working girls, y'understand. Some of my best friends are—"

Stone cut him off to Campbell.

"Anyone in our camp come to mind? She won't have to involve herself with the Colonel, just get him outside for us."

"Zarnov does have a marked inclination for blondes, blondes with long hair," said Campbell thoughtfully, "and there is someone who does come to mind. I'd have to ask her, of course; I couldn't order her to do something like that, but Anna is just free spirited enough to take the deal on."

"Is she trained?" Stone asked cautiously. "I mean we don't want to get someone hurt."

"She's had the training. She's smart and tough . . . and pretty. D'you want to see her?"

"You bet," Hog said quickly.

"All right. I'll have her here tonight."

"What if Zarnov doesn't go for her?"

Campbell almost smirked. "If he doesn't his big Russian reputation isn't worth a plugged kopeck." He put the pipe in his mouth and went out.

When he returned it was late and he had the girl with him. It was cold out and she was wrapped to the eyes in coat and black scarf with a fur hat down to her brows.

"This is Anna," Campbell said. "Anna, meet Mark Stone, Terrance Loughlin, and Hog Wiley."

"I am pleased to meet you," she said with a charming accent. She doffed the fur *shapka* and a cascade of blond hair streamed to her shoulders.

When she opened the coat, Hog whistled. She was dressed in a formfitting blue gown with cleavage; there was no possible question of her gender. She tossed the coat aside.

Loughlin got up and put his hand out. "I'm the one you came to see. May I have this dance?" They waltzed about the room and her laughter tinkled. Campbell puffed his pipe and looked at Stone, who nodded. She was one hell of a woman.

Now, Stone thought, if she could handle an Uzi . . .

When he asked the question, Campbell said, "She is checked out on automatic weapons, pistols, and knives.

She speaks four languages, can drive trucks, and fly planes. I'm not sure if she can cook."

"Sold," Stone said chuckling. "Is she Russian?"

"No. She's a Swede, and wants to go home. She says she's tired of the Soviet Union and I don't blame her." He gathered up his hat and coat. "So am I."

Campbell nodded and left.


The café was very quiet when Mark Stone followed Anna into the room. A doorman, looking like an overdecorated navy admiral, gave them a quick examination from inside the glass doors, then allowed them to enter and deposit their greatcoats in a cloakroom.

It was a large room with a stage at one end behind a circle of footlights. A group of Cossack dancers in high polished boots were performing.

"I have been a lady, and I have gone out evenings," Anna said. "But I've never been a lady of the evening. It should be interesting."

Stone shook his head, amused at the other's eagerness. "Is it okay to speak English here?"

"Oh yes. They expect you to—I mean this place is mostly for tourists, I would imagine. Look at the girls."

They were lined up at the bar, all shapes and sizes, chattering and sipping coffee, their eyes taking in everything and everyone. Several were eyeing him, Stone thought. He looked away. He wanted no truck with hookers.

Anna had them all beat in the looks department anyway, thought Stone, and probably in every other department, too. He liked the lady's style.

Zarnov was not in the room.

They found stools at the bar and ordered coffee; Anna smoked a cigarette. It was agreed that when Zarnov entered, Stone would fade into the background and Anna would make it impossible for the Russian not to notice her.

If he played true to form he would approach her, buy her a drink, and attempt his Russian wiles.

Then, when she went outside with Zarnov and got into a taxi, she would somehow manage to delay their departure until Stone and the others could surround the taxi and drag Zarnov out.

It was a simple plan that ought to work. God willing.

Colonel Zarnov showed up near eleven o'clock, dressed in a dark suit instead of in uniform. When he came through the door, Anna moved toward him with a slinky gait, blond hair down to her shapely shoulders, and he stopped short.

Stone watched from the bar as he stopped her with a remark and she turned toward him, smiling. They began to converse, walked to the bar, and ordered drinks.

The instant Stone was alone, a brunette hooker came his way with a silky skirt that clung like another skin. She nudged Stone with her thigh. "Allo. You give me cigarette, huh?"

He gave her one and lighted it.

"Not tonight, Josephine."

She looked at him, made an odd little noise in her throat, and moved away.

Inside an hour, Zarnov put Anna's coat about her shoulders and they went to the door. Stone caught the quick glance Anna gave him.

He followed, standing in the doorway. The doorman was in the street. Stone eyed the shadows around the café. Hog was to his right and Loughlin his left. Both had seen Zarnov.

The Russian strode into the street, flagged down a

taxi, put the girl into it, and was away in a moment.

The Russian did not get into the cab with her. He slammed the door and the car took off instantly, as if by plan. Stone saw Anna's alarmed face, pale in the window—then she was gone.

In the next instant the street seemed to be filled with armed soldiers. A hundred AK-47s were pointed at his head. Hog and Loughlin were rounded up.

And Zarnov was smiling.

# Chapter Eighteen

In a moment the uniformed men had herded them together, disarmed them, and pushed them into a truck with half a dozen soldiers. No one spoke to them.

The truck took them on a short ride through the streets, into a courtyard, through a short tunnel, and pulled up before a barrackslike building and stopped. The soldiers jumped out and nudged them. An NCO directed them into the building.

Apparently Anna had not been suspected by Zarnov. He had put her in the taxi and it had taken her out of a possible line of fire. The driver had probably brought her back to the café after the ambush was accomplished. Stone hoped it was so, that Zarnov had thought her no more than another hooker.

They were shoved into a barred cell in the half dark; the heavy door slammed on them, and they were alone.

"The sonofabitch ambushed us," Hog said in an annoyed tone.

Loughlin asked, "How did he know we were there?" He frowned at them. "That girl isn't a double agent, huh?"

"She's too pretty for that," Hog said.

"Well, he certainly got her out of the way in a hurry. . ."

Stone shook his head. "I think he's smarter than we gave him credit for. We were so goddamn pleased with our little plan that we didn't think beyond it. Now he's got *us*."

Hog had been inspecting the cell. He shook his head; it was too well built. "Where are we—a police station?"

There were subdued noises in the distance, as if a thick door were between them and others. They were apparently in a holding cell; there was no cot or bench, only the cage. If they wanted to sit, it was the floor or nothing.

They were left alone for an hour or more. Then the lights were turned up, a door opened and closed, and a Russian colonel stood before them, hands in his pockets, a smile of triumph on his face.

"So we have you," he said. "It was only a question of time."

"Everything is," Stone retorted. "Who are you?"

"My name is Zarnov."

Stone shrugged as if he had never heard the name. "Why are we being held here?"

"Because you are saboteurs and spies."

"You don't have to bother with foolishness like proof, huh?" Hog asked.

"No," Zarnov agreed. "The trial will be a technicality. You are here. That's enough." He turned to go, then paused. "By the way, your journalist, Daniels, died last night."

"You mean you killed him?"

"No, he died of an illness."

Stone said, "I'm surprised you admit you have him."

"It doesn't matter now, does it?" Zarnov smiled again. "In a few hours you will follow him."

He rapped on a door; it opened and he went through it.

Loughlin asked, "Do we believe him about Daniels?"

"Of course not." Stone sat down on the floor. "Let's conserve our strength."

The taxi went two blocks before Anna, shouting at the driver, got him to pull over. He explained that he had been paid to take her out of danger. She thanked him and got out of the taxi, intending to find another one. But the driver got out and suddenly grabbed her, struggling to put her back into the cab.

Anna laced her fingers together and brought them down hard on the back of his neck, then gave him a jolting uppercut with her knee. He moaned and fell, sprawling in the gutter.

She jumped in the cab and slammed the door. Yanking the wheel, she shoved down the accelerator and drove back to the café in time to see the trucks rolling away. She followed them and saw one turn into a ministry building drive.

Abandoning the taxi, she ran after the truck. It went past the ministry parking area, through a tunnel, and into a far courtyard.

She watched men take the three Americans out and push them into the building.

Then she went to telephone Byron Campbell.

She gave him the exact address and he said, yes, he knew the building. It was a K.G.B. substation and was thought to be a communications center. He was a little surprised to hear the three had been taken there.

"Being a holding station, security there is practically nil compared to some other places he could have taken Stone and his team. Our Colonel Zarnov is playing it foxy; he wants to feather his own cap, but with those guys he may have outfoxed himself. I hope Stone and his boys have some tricks in mind."

"What about your connections?" Anna asked. "There must be something you can do to help, Mr. Campbell."

"I doubt it." Campbell paused. "We'll watch the building of course, but it'll be guarded. We'll have to see what happens. Don't let Zarnov see you again."

"Right," Anna said. She hung up.

*PRAVDA* REPORTING. *Pravda* reports there is regretfully no news of the American newsman who disappeared recently. Every effort has been made by the Soviet government to locate the missing journalist.

It is now thought that the man, Lee Daniels, was abducted by criminals and his body buried. The American was known to have carried large sums on his person.

The Soviet government will continue the search.

Dr. Lyudin sat behind his desk and leaned back, frowning at his visitor. He took off his horn-rimmed glasses and polished them slowly. His eyes were tiny raisins in a pale face.

"He is much too weak to attempt a further experiment, Colonel."

Zarnov's jaw worked as he gritted his teeth. This little clinical mouse annoyed him and he showed it. But it did not seem to effect Lyudin. It was all he could do to keep from shouting at the man ... but Lyudin was in charge here, K.G.B. or no K.G.B. This was a hospital and his rank had no bearing. If he could manage to pull the patient out—but that was another story.

"When will he be strong enough, comrade Doctor?"

"I cannot say for certain. The drug works differently on people."

"But you knew that ..."

Lyudin finished polishing and put the glasses on. "May I remind you, Colonel, you were the one who insisted on drugging the patient."

"He is an enemy of the state!"

"That is no concern of mine. My single concern is medical. My report will state I do not concur in the drugging and I insist that the patient be allowed to recover his strength before another demand is made upon it."

"But—"

Lyudin's voice turned hard. "No matter what crimes he has committed against the state, we are not executioners! I will not kill this man for you!"

Zarnov got up. He stared at the doctor, his face red, then he stomped out, slamming the door.

Lyudin smiled.


Zarnov made sure the paperwork was in order. He presented it in its duplicates to the office staff, had a short interview with the general commanding the substation, and received at last his certificates which allowed him to transport the three American criminals back to Moscow for trial.

Of course they would never arrive.

At the motor pool he demanded three large trucks for his prisoners and guards. But only one truck was available. The motor pool officer was adamant. He could not spare three trucks for a journey to Moscow. When would they be returned? His trucks were constantly under repair as it was and he was forever short-handed.

Zarnov tried to go over the man's head and was refused.

He finally had to take what he could get, one truck and one small staff car that would carry four men.

Nine men were assigned him, including four drivers who would take turns at the wheels. They were all middle-aged people; a few were veterans of the Afghanistan troubles.

His itinerary showed stopping places each night. Night was when the three would be killed trying to escape. Probably the third night. He would arrange it that way, and it should go like clockwork. His NCO, Galina, was a short, very compact female who enjoyed that sort of thing and who had the additional blessing of being able to keep her mouth tight shut; they had worked together in the past—to her advantage.

The third night they would stop in rolling forest country. After the others were asleep, Galina would quietly take the prisoners out of their cell. She would give them the idea that she was helping them so they would go with her without a fuss. She would promise to take their shackles off when they got into the woods. The stopping place was a compound of wooden buildings with a low wall surrounded by forest.

But when they got into the woods, she would give them each a burst with her automatic rifle. Then remove their leg shackles.

Colonel Zarnov would then commend her for alert-

ness and for devotion to duty. No one escaped while
Galina was present. She could see in the dark.

The bodies would be loaded on the truck and they
would continue to Moscow.

The Soviet diplomats would then present their regrets
to the American authorities saying it was deplorable that
the accused men chose to make an escape attempt rather
than face a trial. The guard had no choice but to shoot.


Hours passed. Without a watch, Stone thought, it
would be difficult to tell the time of day in the dark
building. All the windows were covered and only one
dim unshaded bulb burned just outside the cell.

The room they had been placed in had obviously
been made over from something else, a barracks, perhaps. Their cage was separated from the rest by a ceil-
ing-high partition, painted gray. Outside the cage,
against the partition, was a bench, a single chair and a
rickety-looking table with nothing on it. The bench was
gray, the table and chair black. The floor was bare
boards, unpainted or stained.

Inside the cage other previous prisoners had
scratched and written words and phrases. All were in
Russian but for three lonely words: Lenin eats shit.

Apparently the guards had not yet noticed the English letters.

It was near midnight by Stone's watch when the door
opened suddenly, another light was turned on to make
the area garish, and two guards and a woman stood in
the open door. They were obviously arguing in Russian.
The woman was very strident and harsh. She was
dressed in a short white coat, had a white shirt and black
tie under it, and was in dark pants. There was a stetho-
scope about her neck and she carried a heavy clipboard.

Her hair was drawn back from her face in a severe bun at the nape of her neck and for more than a minute Stone did not recognize her. It was Anna!

Hog gulped, recognizing her a moment later and kicked Loughlin, whispering, "Anna!"

Loughlin stared. "You sure?"

She was obviously commanding the guards to open the cell, and after more argument they reluctantly assented. One threw up his hands and disappeared, while the other pulled the AK off his shoulder. In a flood of Russian, Anna assailed him, then pushed him aside and spoke to the prisoners in the cell, her voice as imperious as it had been with the guards. But her words were different.

"We have no time at all to get out of here. There is a car waiting. You must put these two in the cell."

She turned away as the first man returned with a huge ring and began to select a key. Anna kept him off-guard with her constant chiding. His fingers were trembling as he put the key in the lock and turned it.

The first man leveled his rifle at the prisoners.

As the door opened, Anna said, "Now!" She suddenly slashed at the man with the rifle, hitting him in the throat with the edge of the heavy clipboard. It was expertly done and he went down with a gargling sound. She grabbed the rifle from his arms.

Hog grabbed the other and hurled him against the concrete wall of the cell. He crashed into it and fell with a groan.

Loughlin pulled the other man into the cell and locked it.

"This way!" Anna called.

They ran through the open door. The room was a kind of office, with two desks and a rifle rack. Stone caught up an AK that was slung over a chairback. Hog pulled two from the rack and heaved one to Loughlin, who grinned.

Anna was in the hallway, heading for the door, and Stone ran after her. Twenty yards from the door, it opened and three guards came in, chattering. They halted, mouths open as they caught sight of Anna with the rifle.

She slid to a halt and the rifle stuttered.

The three fell like ninepins; glass shattered on the doors and the sounds echoed in the corridor like thunder. Blood sprayed the walls.

Stone heard Loughlin say, "Jesus! What a gal!"

They sped through the doors and down the steps, where an idling blue Volga was waiting.

They threw themselves, in Anna taking the wheel, pulling out before the doors were closed. Someone yelled behind them and a shot was fired. Hog leaned out and the AK-47 spat viciously. Stone heard more glass shatter, then they were in the tunnel.

Anna gave the car the petrol and turned into the broad street as the tires protested. A siren began to wail behind them.

Stone said, "Get off this street, lady." He looked around at them. "Everybody all right?"

"We ain't sleepy no more," Hog said. "You sure make a doozie of a doc, honey."

"Thanks. It was the only thing I could think of in a hurry."

"Well, it worked," Stone replied. "What did you tell those guards anyway?"

She spun the wheel and turned into a dark street.

"I told them I was from K.G.B. headquarters. I made up some story about a general who wanted to make sure of their physical condition—just for the record. They kept saying it didn't matter, you were going to be shot in a couple of hours. I said I had orders and swore at them a little."

"We're being followed," Hog remarked. "There's red lights back there."

Anna took a corner too fast and the tires screeched.

"Motorcycles," Hog said, growling. "Gimme some room to fire."

"Bust out the rear window," Stone told him.

Hog slammed the butt of the rifle at the glass, shattering it. He fired a burst and swore. "Damn hard to hit—"

Bullets rapped into the car. Anna swerved and took another corner.

Loughlin squirmed around and he and Hog fired together and Hog chuckled. "One down. The other's dropping back."

"He'll try to shadow us," Stone said. "Slow the car —see if you can knock him out."

Anna let up on the pedal and the car slowed immediately. Hog fired a long burst, aiming carefully.

"Did you get him?"

"Can't tell. The light went out, but he may be sneaky."

Anna speeded up again.

Anna said, "We can't go very far in this car with no back window. The police will stop us on sight."

"Who's car is it?" Hog asked.

Anna shrugged. "No idea. We were in a hurry and needed one."

"We understand that," Stone remarked. "We've been stealing cars ever since we came to Russia. The cops probably think a gang of car thieves is at work. Can we drove close to the apartment and ditch the car?"

"I'll try."

It took most of an hour, creeping and speeding by turns, running at times with lights out.

Byron Campbell was waiting for them outside the apartment. "I was worried sick about Anna," he told them, hugging her. "You did it!"

"She was terrific," Stone said. "She makes a great doctor."

Hog agreed. "She can operate on me anytime."

Campbell wanted to hear every detail. They broke out a bottle of vodka and related it all.

Zarnov received a rebuke from his superiors.

One of the two guards was dead, the other badly injured by contact with the cement wall. His jaw was wired so he could not talk. He wrote answers laboriously, saying that a K.G.B. doctor had demanded entrance to the cell to evaluate the prisoners' physical condition. But as he opened the cell door he was violently attacked.

He was not surprised to learn that the other guard was dead and the doctor kidnapped.

# Chapter Nineteen

And in the midst of celebrating their escape, Campbell told them other news. One of his agents, a male nurse who worked in the hospital, had ascertained that a prisoner was indeed being held in the old prison ward.

He had been told this by a man who had served the prisoner meals. The prisoner was not a Russian.

"Ask him for a drawing of the place," Stone said.

"Yes, I already did. However, he says it's impossible. Too many guards. He says we'd never be able to get the man out alive."

"Is he a military man?" Stone asked.

Campbell laughed. "He's a nurse. But I do think it might be difficult for three men to fight thirty or forty who have automatic weapons."

"We've done it before," Hog said.

"I must tell you one more thing. That it is my duty to report that in my opinion Lee Daniels is being held in

Paschenko Hospital prison ward. I must serve my government, you know."

"Can you hold up the sending of that for a day or so?"

The other nodded. "For a short time."

The drawing came from the nurse and Campbell presented it to them, a very crude depiction of the buildings and grounds, with doors drawn in and an indication of the surrounding fence.

They drove around the hospital with Anna at the wheel, to inspect the fence, finding it partly chain link and partly stone. There was barbed wire atop some of it but not all.

Anna said she thought they had begun to put up the barbed wire when they used the prison ward. But since its disuse they had not bothered with the rest.

She said, "We know that prisoners are held at a different place, but that's all we know."

When they got back to the apartment Stone said, "We'll go over the wall tonight—agreed?"

Hog and Loughlin nodded.

"We do it quick and dirty and get out before they realize what's going down." He looked at Anna. "We need some rope, about seventy feet of it."

"Can do."

"And three-pronged hooks for the ends."

She said, "I'll ask Campbell. He can find anything in Russia. That's it?"

"Unless you can get us some grenades."

"I'll ask." She went to the door and out.

Campbell was a miracle worker. The rope and hooks were no problem, but he also brought them a box of fragmentation grenades that he said had been stolen months back from an army unit.

"It says on the box they're three-second fuses, so watch it."

Hog was delighted to get them. There were times when nothing worked as well as a grenade.

Campbell hung around till well after dark, saying he would drive them to the hospital himself. Anna wanted to but he overruled her. "I'm the chief. You're just an Indian. You stay in the tepee."

She growled at him under her breath.

An hour after midnight Campbell dropped them off at the north wall of the hospital. He would return every fifteen minutes. The wall was stone, about eighteen feet high with no barbed wire coils at its top.

Across the rutted street was a silent factory building. They stood in the deep shadow of the wall adjusting equipment, then Hog tossed the first hook up. It made a metallic clang, not too loud, and Hog went up hand over hand. He sat on the top of the wall, looked around, and motioned. Stone and Loughlin tossed the hooks up as Hog pulled up the rope, refastened the hook, and dropped to the far side.

Stone dropped down, finding himself in a pebbled area. A few feet away was an automobile park with several dark shapes. Probably cars belonging to doctors, he thought. They had been there for a time; their windshields were misted over.

Behind the park was the administration building—it was so marked on the map. Most of the lights were out. Beyond it was the building they were after.

With Loughlin in the lead, they crossed the parking area to the side of the dark building. Close to the building they could hear music coming from somewhere above.

Loughlin moved to the end and beckoned. Stone

craned his neck, looking around the corner. The area between the buildings was lighted . . . not brightly, but enough to see well. Several men were sitting far to their right, talking and smoking.

"Nurses, off duty," Loughlin said.

"Haven't seen no guards," Hog whispered. "Maybe they don't guard this place."

Stone pointed to their left. A squat weapons carrier was parked at the end of the building. It was empty, with lights out. "Maybe they ride around in that."

The building facing them had bars on the second floor. But no lights. Was Daniels up there?

They waited ten minutes but the talkers did not move. Two men came out of the building next to them and got in the weapons carrier, started the engine, and roared off in the opposite direction.

Stone said, "So they make a round maybe once an hour." It was just one-thirty by his watch. "Let's go around those guys."

Hog went in the lead, making a wide circle to keep out of the line of sight of the smokers. They went completely around a long ward building and approached the prison ward from the other side. Once the weapons carrier came near and they all flattened themselves on the ground and were not noticed.

The building had three doors, one on each end and one in the middle. There was a light on over the door and Hog walked up to it bold as brass and tried the handle. It was locked.

As they started for the middle door several men in white coats came out of another building and walked along a path, chatting, and approached the middle door.

Stone said quickly, "We go in with them."

With Hog in the lead, they ran over a grassy plot and

approached the men from behind. There were three, two rather fat and one skinny black-haired man with glasses. One of the fat men took out a key ring and inserted the key in the lock as Hog stepped up behind him and leveled the AK rifle.

The three turned in astonishment and the fat man dropped the keys. The skinny one said something in Russian and Stone shook his head.

Loughlin picked up the keys and handed them to the transfixed fat man, who took them as if they were red hot.

Hog pushed open the door and Stone said, "Shall we all go in?"

"You are English!" the skinny man said in surprise. "What do you want here?" He stared at the guns.

"You have a prisoner."

The skinny man shook his head. "He is not here."

One of the fat men asked questions in Russian and Hog prodded him with the rifle and he shut up.

Mark said, annoyed, "Why isn't he here?"

"They moved him today!"

"Shit!" Hog growled.

"Take us to the cell," Stone said gruffly. "Let's go."

Their footsteps echoed in the corridor. Was the building empty?

The skinny man said, "The prison ward is upstairs." He pointed to a sign with an arrow.

"Why is the building empty?" Stone asked.

"We had orders to move everyone out. Planeloads of men are coming from Afghanistan—burn victims. We must care for them here."

They went up the stairs. The barred door was standing open and there was no one in any of the cells.

Loughlin pushed the fat men into one of the cells and locked it despite their protests.

"Who was the prisoner?" Stone asked.

The skinny man shrugged. "An American. I was told he was a newsman."

"Where did they take him?"

"I do not know, but an air force truck came for him."

They put the man into another of the cells. He went philosophically. They would find him in the morning, he said.

Campbell picked them up when they went back over the wall, disappointed that they were alone. Stone explained what they had learned. "Is there an air base nearby?"

"Yes," said Campbell, frowning. "There's one not far from here at all."

"Then that," Stone growled, "is our next stop."

Loughlin asked, "Why would they use an air base?"

"Maybe because it was handy—and it's got a brig."


Lee Daniels had been hustled out of the cell and downstairs into a waiting truck. He still felt queasy from the drugs and he had eaten very little for several days.

Around him were other trucks and vans; the entire hospital seemed to be moving. Patients were carried out and put into ambulances, other equipment was carried in . . . Dr. Lyudin, when he'd talked to him last, had said the people were making way for a burn ward. Other facilities had proven inadequate and Paschenko was being pressed into service. Because of the Afghanistan adventure, more medical wards were needed.

He was able to lie down and close his eyes. The truck drove through the city and beyond. Daniels paid no attention. They would do what they would do.

His hope was growing dim; he was probably forgotten.

He did not stir when the truck slowed and came to a stop. He could hear voices and commands; then the truck moved on, more slowly, for several miles and finally halted, backed up, and the driver switched off.

Daniels sat up slowly as the back doors were opened and a man motioned him to come. They helped him down and he was led into a gray building, past desks where uniformed men were working, into a dim corridor that smelled dank, and finally into a row of cells.

"Be it ever so humble," Daniels said as they pushed him into one.

The cell had a cot and a toilet. It was big enough to turn around in, but not much more. He sat on the cot and put his head in his hands.

# Chapter Twenty

Senator Harler called in John Davison and they sat with cups and coffee between them. "John, what is the situation with Mark Stone and the others? Have you been in communication with them?"

"No sir. The last information we had was that Stone and his men were leaving for Leningrad."

"Lee Daniels was taken there?"

"We are sure of it, sir. I've had a communication with the C.I.A chief there, Byron Campbell. He reported several days ago that in his opinion Daniels was held in Paschenko Hospital under drugs."

"Paschenko." Harler frowned. "Tass gave out an item about Paschenko only a few days ago."

"Yes sir. They were touting a new burn center if you remember. The situation with Daniels changes or could change daily. They've moved him several times—that's what makes it so difficult. By the time Stone and his men find out where he is and make plans to get to him, the Russkis move him."

"Yes. It's damned inconvenient." He tapped a tooth with a finger. "I know they're in considerable danger . . . I wish to hell we could do something about that."

Davison nodded. "We are dead sure that if the K.G.B. locates Stone and the others—" He drew a finger across his throat. "They will simply be eliminated. They will disappear and the Soviet authorities will deny all knowledge. As you know, sir, they are good at that."

"Yes. With no possibility of a trial."

Davison chuckled. "Trial! The only trial they'll get is with an AK-47. They can't admit they have Daniels— it's all touchy as hell."

"I would dearly love to make a stink about this." Harler sighed deeply. "And the first thing I'd like is to strangle that goddamned Zarnov."

"We think that because Zarnov has had to keep moving Daniels he hasn't been able to dig much out of him . . . if anything at all. Interrogation of a hostile witness does take time. Campbell seems to feel that Stone and his men are on Daniels's heels."

"God, let's hope so!"

Stone and his team dropped off the C.I.A man and continued on in his car.

It was about a five-mile drive to the air base. The main gate was on one of the two roads that ran past it and the two sentries stared at them suspiciously as they drove slowly by.

It was necessary to make a wide circle then to return to the base without driving past the gate again. There was no traffic at all; the police would probably stop them on sight. There were very few houses near the base and no place to park the car.

It was necessary to run it under a copse of trees a mile or more away, then return on foot.

They were on the south side of the base, where there was no road, only open fields with few and scattered trees. It was a formidable fence on this side, actually two fences with a ten-foot space in between. Barbed wire was woven into it, and without bolt cutters, there was no possibility of getting through it.

As they studied it, a jeep appeared far off in the distance, a bright light moving ahead of it. They faded back into the field and lay flat. In several minutes the jeep moved past with the light sweeping from side to side methodically.

"We maybe could dig under it," Hog remarked. "But they'd see the hole."

"I wonder if it's this way all around the field?" Stone said. "I vote we go up to the west side and look."

They reached the southwest corner of the base before the jeep came around again with its busy light. There was a handy ditch not far off and they waited till the sentries were past.

The fence was not the same. There was only a single barrier instead of two, but with barbed wire coiled along the top. The Russkis really wanted no visitors. The welcome mat was not out.

"We are jolly well not getting in," Loughlin said. "Not without some equipment."

"And when we get in, where do we go?"

"Over there, where those buildings are," Hog said. "He's in one of 'em, huh?"

They walked along the fence to decide where the best way in might be—when they returned with bolt cutters.

The tower lights were ineffective and easy to avoid. No one challenged them or fired on them. Loughlin suggested the towers were not even manned at night.

They had to dodge the patrol jeep one more time as they returned to the Volga under the trees.

Zarnov was called to the K.G.B. building on Dzerzhinsky Square. His immediate superior, General Vladimir Belov, was in a snit. Nothing had been forthcoming from the American, Daniels. The American ambassador had been sarcastic and disbelieving by turns. Every meeting with him was worse than the last and Belov's nerves were worn thin.

The lies that Belov had to mouth were dry as dust in his throat and he could see the disgust in the ambassador's eyes.

But there had been something of value brought to him. And he summoned Zarnov to see it. Zarnov had reported that three American mercenaries had come into the Soviet Union in the American Senator Harler's retinue.

Belov had discovered who they were.

He had the photos taken by Soviet Customs, and he had photos taken in Southeast Asia. These had been purchased at a considerable price from a secret agent in Paris. The three mercenaries were the same. And Zarnov, when he looked at them, was filled with rage. These three had caused him intolerable problems and considerable harsh treatment from higher-ups. It had been suggested that perhaps he was getting senile and could no longer be trusted with important secret matters.

Even Belov had an acid tongue concerning the three. Zarnov had not been able to bring to earth three foreigners who did not even speak the language!

The commandos were in the Soviet Union to rescue the American, Lee Daniels. They had made several attempts already and were probably on Daniels's track at this moment.

"The American is at an air base now, General. There is no way they could know where he has been taken."

"They seem to have sources."

"Yes, the C.I.A. is undoubtedly helping them, but we know those agents and are keeping watch on them. Sooner or later they will lead us to the mercenaries."

"Let us hope you are right this time." Belov fingered the photos. "The Americans do not admit these men are in the Soviet Union. Therefore when you find them you will not capture them. Is that understood? You will bury them and that will be an end of it. The Americans will not be able to protest."

"It will be the greatest pleasure I have ever had—when it is accomplished. I have marked these men for death. They will not escape me."

"Do not underestimate them."

Zarnov nodded. He left the meeting still raging. The three mercenaries had made a fool of him in front of his superiors. He would never forgive them for that; he would follow them to the ends of the earth to even the score.

He flew to the air base at once and when he inquired after the political prisoner, he was shown to the office of Dr. Soslan Gritsenko, Chief of Physicians.

"Why am I here?" Zarnov asked.

"I understand you are in charge of the prisoner." Gritsenko was a burly man, bearded, with thin-rimmed spectacles on a fleshy nose. His clothes were rumpled but he exuded authority.

"Yes, that is so."

Gritsenko regarded him as if he were an object on a slide, ready to be put into a microscope. "The man is dehydrated and weak. The revolution does not allow torture, Colonel."

"He has not been tortured!"

"So you say. I do not agree with your medical opinion." Gritsenko's words were heavy with sarcasm. "I have given orders that you will not be allowed to see the prisoner. You may—"

"You have no right to do that!"

"Oh?" Gritsenko's mouth turned down. "Look about you, Colonel. You are not at K.G.B. headquarters now. I will give the medical orders here."

"The man is a secret prisoner! He is an enemy of the state!"

"So long as he is on this post he is under my care. You will be informed when he can be moved."

Zarnov gritted his teeth. The infernal insolence of the medical staffs! He stormed from the room, slamming doors.

But he was not allowed to see the prisoner. When he called General Belov and explained, the general called Dr. Gritsenko and discovered the doctor had the right to care for a patient on the air base, regardless of his rank or position. The regulations provided for this.

And neither could General Belov have the prisoner moved from the base without the written permission of Dr. Gritsenko.

Stalemate.

# Chapter Twenty-one

Campbell provided a pair of bolt cutters and four camouflage fatigues—where he got them was a mystery. He came for them well after dark and drove them to the air base in a Toyota van.

He let them out a mile away and they trudged across a field to get to the fence, guided by the blinking lights.

Their plan was a daring one. Stone hoped it would work. He was not a praying man, but he said a little prayer to the god of idiots and those of mean capacity, those who would put themselves into the enemy's hands.

It was very dark at the edge of the field where the brush had been cleared away. The flashing lights from the tower a hundred yards or more away came and went at intervals. The light swept the ground unhurriedly, making a continuous circle.

Loughlin timed it; the light came every twenty seconds and lasted about four. In between, the periods of darkness seemed very much darker.

On his knees by the wire fence, Stone used the bolt cutters. He sliced the wire in a neat rectangle, two feet wide and three high. It took half a dozen pauses to do it, lying flat as the light swept by.

Finished, he pulled the section of wire out and tossed it aside with the cutters. He crawled through the hole with Anna at his heels. They lay flat as the light passed over them.

Hog and Loughlin crawled through and the Briton said, "The jeep ought to be here in five minutes."

Stone nodded, peering to his left. They were about to take a calculated risk—give themselves up. If it worked, they would be in the brig with Daniels. If not . . . He'd rather not think about that.

But if the men in the jeep fired at them, it would be difficult. Then they'd have a fight on their hands. Each of them carried five frag grenades . . . their only weapons. They would have to use them if it came to a fight. If not, they'd leave the grenades behind in the grass.

Except that each of them had a grenade taped to his ankle.

They were counting on hasty searches. When the Russians found they were carrying no weapons, the searches might be less thorough.

"Here she comes," Hog growled. He had opposed the plan from the beginning. Hog hated to give up anything. And it made him nervous, he said, to go into the enemy's camp unarmed.

Headlights appeared far to their left, coming from behind a row of trees and sheds at the far end of the runway. The three-man jeep would come along the road that paralleled the fence.

They would allow themselves to be seen—as if they were a group of rank amateurs. The tower light would pick them out and the jeep would do the rest.

And hopefully a machine gunner would hold his fire. That was the touchy area.

But Byron Campbell had said: "This is not wartime and the sentries have orders—I am reliably informed— not to fire unless they are fired upon."

Stone asked, "Who informed you?"

"Sources," Campbell said. "Sources." He chewed his pipe stem. "They will want to question you, not put a lily in your hands. Stand with your hands up and do not run."

"You can't trust the bastards," Hog said in a growly voice. "Remember that Korean airliner?"

"Well," Campbell said, making a face. "You can go in with guns and see how far you get. In this particular case I think guile is better than guns."

"Of course you aren't going, dear," Anna said.

"And neither are you," Stone told her.

She flared instantly. "Of course I am!"

Stone regarded her with surprise. They had argued and talked for hours, hammering out the plan, and fi- nally agreed on it—even Hog had reluctantly voted for it—and now Anna wanted to go along!

"You cannot go," he said firmly.

"Why—because I'm a female?"

"Well . . ."

"I can shoot as well as any of you. I can probably run faster! I can see in the dark—"

"She can argue pretty good too," put in Campbell. "She can also speak Russian."

"And French, and Swedish!"

Stone fell back on: "We don't need another person on the raid."

Hog remarked, "If the Russkis find out you're a

woman they'll put you somewhere else. You won't be with us."

"They won't find out! I'll dress the same as you. They won't undress me on the spot!"

Campbell said, "You already know she's good at disguise. Remember, she played the doctor bit."

"But we don't need—"

"You can use me! Stop the arguments! Let's go over the plan again."

"Well, she *does* speak the lingo," Loughlin said. "It might come in handy."

"And there's one other thing," Campbell remarked, puffing smoke. "The K.G.B. is looking for *three* of you. With Anna you'll be four. That may confuse them just a little. It's possible they may not figure you for *who* you are until it's too late."

Stone sighed and looked at the others. Loughlin smiled and Hog shrugged.

Loughlin reached out and fingered her long blond hair. "How're you going to hide this?"

"I'll cut it off short, like yours."

Hog said, "You sure you want to do that, honey?"

She smiled at him. "It'll grow back. Who's got the scissors?"

So she had come along, with no makeup and a little mud on her cheeks.


They all jumped up as the jeep approached, as if they had just come through the wire. The searchlight pinned them and all hands went up; they stood still.

The jeep approached at high speed and braked hard, slewing around. Two men jumped out with automatic rifles pointing. They yelled commands.

Anna whispered, "They ask who we are."

Stone shrugged, hands held palms upward. "No comprendo."

The driver of the jeep was apparently in command. He stood, leaning on the windscreen, a big rough-looking farmer type. He barked a command and the riflemen searched them quickly, overlooking the taped grenades.

One of them investigated the cut fence and they held a rapid-fire conversation. One tossed the bolt cutters into the jeep. But they missed the grenades in the grass.

Then they were pushed into a line and the way pointed out to them. They marched across a field with the jeep following.

Anna, behind Stone, whispered, "They don't know what to make of us."

They had not noticed her gender. She did not look at all like a beautiful woman.

The jeep driver had radioed ahead and they were met by an NCO and half a dozen soldiers with rifles and bayonets attached. These men surrounded them in a very businesslike manner and the NCO spoke in French asking who they were.

Stone shook his head.

The man tried halting English.

Loughlin, in his best British accent, said, "We demand to see the British authorities."

The NCO was astonished. "You British!?"

"Certainly, old sod."

"What you do here?" The NCO looked them up and down.

"It was a game, old boy," Stone said.

Loughlin broadened his accent. "We thought it would be a jolly adventure, you know. Just to see if we could do it. You understand?"

The Russian shook his head in disbelief. His expression said he was undoubtedly facing a group of hare-brained idiots. An officer came out of a nearby building and the NCO quickly related what he knew and the officer stared at them.

His English was very good. "You cut a hole in the fence?"

"Just for laughs," Loughlin said. "Nothing serious."

The NCO showed him the bolt cutters.

Loughlin quickly said, "We'll gladly pay for any damage, sir."

The officer's expression closely resembled the NCO's. "Why did you do this?"

Loughlin smiled winningly. "To protest the Soviet position on human rights."

The officer shook his head, then made up his mind. He spoke to the NCO and pointed to the nearest building. The NCO marched them inside. A man opened the barred door of a large cage and they were pushed in. The door slammed shut and the NCO went back outside. They heard him shouting to the soldiers.

Anna said, "He's telling them to return to barracks."

They were in a brick building with stucco walls. The cage faced a large office room that was divided into various smaller rooms by chest-high partitions. The man who had put them in the cage sat at one desk with a small bulb burning. The rest of the room was dim.

"This is the right building," Stone said. "It's the base jail. Daniels is in here somewhere."

Hog said, "This guy is the night orderly." He indicated the man at the desk. "He's got the key to this cage on his belt."

"Call him over," Loughlin said. "I'll grab him."

Stone beckoned Hog. "You've been in more jails than the rest of us, what's likely here?"

Hog winked at Anna. "He tryin' to make me feel good." To Stone he said, "What you got here is your typical two-bit stucco hoosegow. It's just a crackerbox because they probably don't have anything but drunks in it." He pointed to the office. "That's where they book 'em, and back there," he jerked his thumb, "is the jail part. There'll be a corridor and cells off it."

"How many locked doors?"

Hog pursed his lips. "Probably one, not counting this one and the cell doors. There'll be a door to the corridor."

"How many jailers?"

"They don't need but two. This one and the guy back there. He'll be in an alcove or something through that door." He pointed to a heavy door at the back of the office.

"And the guy back there will have keys?"

"Yep. You get him and you got it."

Stone nodded. He frowned at the Russian at the desk. He was perhaps fifteen feet away, his back to them, doubtless writing a report.

There were hundreds of papers pinned to the walls and some kind of equipment beyond the man at the desk; it glowed with a greenish light and pinged now and then.

They would never have a better time to get out.

"I think I can get our guard to come closer," Anna said.

"He's not dumb enough to come close enough for us to reach him."

"I can get him to come closer than he is . . ." Her voice became seductive.

Hog grinned at her. "Okay, honey. If you can get him to come a little closer—just a little closer . . ."

She said to Stone, "I give him a strip-tease. Maybe he'll get careless, yes?"

"It's the only bloody chance we've got. Let's give her a little strip-tease music."

Stone glanced at Hog, nodding.

They began to clap hands softly. "Take it off, take it off, take it off . . ."

The Russian looked around at them in surprise, then went back to his writing.

When he heard Anna's voice his heard jerked up. He stared at them in astonishment and they could read his mind. There was a woman in the cell! How could that be?

Anna was watching him, smiling at him.

The guard rose, licking his lips. He counted them, four. He had not noticed that one was a woman! He stepped closer to the cell and halted.

The woman was peeling the fatigues off her shoulder. Her tawny skin gleamed in the dim light. He suddenly realized what a woman this was!

He took several steps closer—don't get too close! He stared, grinning, as she pushed the fatigues down farther, showing a bit of pink nipple and the roundness of a breast.

The sight fascinated him. And it was his last.

Hog's knife quivered in his throat, the steel buried almost to the hilt. The man jerked, reached to pluck out the offending metal, and dropped to his knees. His eyes rolled up and he fell sidelong, collapsing on the hard floor.

Loughlin reached a long arm through the bars, fingers clawing. But the body was too far to reach. He swore.

Stone whipped off his web belt. "See if this will catch . . ."

Loughlin tossed the belt, buckle first, trying to snag anything, but it would not catch.

Anna said, "Fasten two belts together."

"Hell, all four belts," Hog growled. "Make a god-damn rope."

It took a few minutes to fasten them together and Loughlin tried again . . . and again.

Stone found himself holding his breath. At any moment someone could come into the office and see what had happened.

The belt-rope slid over the man's body and rattled on the floor. Loughlin tossed it again and this time it caught in a loop on the man's shoulder. The Briton rolled the body on its back, a few inches nearer.

Several more tosses and the belt caught on the pistol holster and, as Loughlin pulled gently, the body slowly rolled. An arm flopped toward them and Hog reached through the bars and pulled the body close.

Stone had the key ring in his hands in a second. There were eight keys on the brass ring. The cage door clicked open at the fifth try.

They dragged the body inside and closed the door.

Stone gave the keys to Loughlin. "You and Anna get Daniels. Hog and I'll get guns." He picked the Russian's pistol out of the holster and slipped it into his belt. Loughlin and Anna ran to the back metal door. Loughlin picked an AK off the wall.

The inner guard looked around in astonishment as Loughlin came through the door. He grabbed at his pistol and Loughlin shot him twice.

Anna yelled, "Mr. Daniels—where are you?"

A startled voice answered, "I'm here . . . in the third cell!"

# Chapter Twenty-two

Zarnov quickly mustered strength. He explained matters to General Belov, who enlisted General Yedensky, and an imperative call went out to the chief of physicians ordering him to turn over the prisoner, Daniels, to Colonel Zarnov at once.

Zarnov would leave Moscow immediately and come to the air base with his credentials and claim his prisoner. There would be no interference.

Or heads would roll.

Anna opened the barred door with the fourth key and ran to the cell. Daniels was sitting on the edge of an iron cot, staring in disbelief at her. "Who are you?"

She glanced at him as she shoved the key into the lock. He looked haggard and thin, with deep lines in his face. He was pale as paper and even in the dim light she could see his hands tremble.

"We've come to get you out of here," she told him. She called for Loughlin to come and help.

Daniels could not stand unaided. They put his arms about their shoulders and pulled him from the cell. A prisoner in another cell yelled at them and shook the bars. Anna told him to shut up.

They walked him into the office where Hog and Stone were checking rifles and shoving extra clips into pockets and belts.

Daniels asked, "You came to get me?"

Loughlin grinned at him. "Don't you want to go?"

Daniels began to laugh . . . then choke, and tears came to his eyes.

Hog said, "You were missing in action, pal. M.I.A. And you're looking at the M.I.A. Hunters."

Stone went to the door as Anna slung an AK over her shoulder. Opening it, he peered at the dark field; the tower lights were still making their monotonous sweeps. Daniels looked terrible, his eyes sunken and skin sallow, and he was weak as a noodle. Had the damned Russkis withheld food from him?

Off to the right were three parked trucks, lined up neatly beside a weapons carrier. He pointed to them. "We grab a truck, okay?"

"Piece of cake," Loughlin said.

"All right." Stone went out. "Single file, let's go."

Loughlin went first and Stone brought up the rear. Hog and Anna half carried the journalist.

Loughlin halted suddenly and motioned them back against the buildings. They stood motionless and a small truck rattled from between two buildings, heading out into the open field and across the runway.

As it passed them, Loughlin motioned again and

went on. The parked trucks were about a hundred yards away.

They came to a low building with a wide open door. Inside, men were working under bright lights, hammering and boring. Metal sparks were flying as a crew worked on a large truck. An engine was chugging as men yelled.

Loughlin looked back and Stone motioned him on. There was no way to go around this building. They had to chance the open door.

But as they passed it a man stepped out. He was hatless, stopping to light a cigarette—then to stare at them. He was dressed in a uniform under coveralls.

He said something to them and Anna replied briefly. They kept walking.

The man snapped a command at them.

Anna said, "He says to halt."

Stone barked, "Then halt." He was closest to the man. He stepped back quickly and flipped the butt of the rifle up. It hit the man under the chin a hard blow. He caught the Russian as he fell.

Anna said, "He is an officer!"

There was a yell from inside the building and Stone turned. Several men were pointing at him, and one started to run toward him.

Stone yanked the grenade from his ankle and tossed it into the doorway. Jumping back to the shelter of the outside he caught the grenade that Hog flipped him. The grenade inside exploded. He tossed the second one after it. As it exploded, Loughlin snapped, "That's torn it."

"Run for the trucks," Stone called.

A flare went up from one of the towers. It shot into the dark sky and exploded into a greenish glare, lighting up the entire field. At the same time a siren began wailing.

The small truck that had gone into the field made a wide circle and started back and a searchlight flicked on. Loughlin fired a burst with the AK and the light went out. The truck stopped as if it had hit a wall. Another flare arced up.

Then Anna yelled and pointed between two buildings. "This way!"

Eighty or ninety yards away was a helicopter.

"Come on!"

Shots cracked by them. Someone was firing from behind.

Stone yelled, "Forget the trucks. Hit the chopper!" Turning, he fired a long burst at their pursuers.

Anna tossed him her rifle and sprinted ahead. There were dark, windowless buildings on both sides. Beyond the chopper was a light plane and beyond it another helicopter. Anna was climbing in the first chopper.

Hog picked up Daniels bodily and ran toward the aircraft.

Loughlin and Stone faced about, waiting. As a half dozen pursuers came around the corner they were silhouetted against one of the greenish flares. Loughlin pulled the pin and tossed his grenade toward them. He and Stone hit the deck. When it exploded, they were up and running for the chopper.

The rotor was spinning. Anna knelt in the doorway and fired over their heads.

Bullets cracked past and several rapped into the side of the chopper. Loughlin dived at the doorway and Hog pulled him in. Stone followed, headfirst.

Instantly the chopper lifted, Hog Wiley at the controls.

They banked away, only a dozen feet off the ground, and the chopper raced between buildings.

Stone took over the heavy machine gun from Anna. He sent bursts back, smashing into the other helicopter and the plane. Hog lifted over the left building and dropped down again. Directly ahead was a line of choppers.

Hog yelped happily and commenced triggering the chopper's 40mm cannon and rockets.

Stone watched the streams of fire pound each airship in turn as they passed over. The first exploded into a giant ball of fire—then the second, and the concussion lifted them. All the choppers were burning.

They rapidly gained altitude. Looking back, Stone could see only destruction. Even one of the buildings was on fire. Men, like ants, were running about and Hog was laughing. "Damn, let's go back and do 'er again!" he yelled above the thundering roar of the HINDS gunship in flight.

Anna shouted for someone to come and look at the map.

Stone moved beside her. There was a map case beside the seat and he opened it and flipped through, finding one that detailed the area they were in. Finland was less than 150 miles away to the east. He gave Hog a heading.

With the air base behind them, the chopper dropped low, just above the treetops for concealment. In the dark confusion it might be difficult for an observer to tell in which direction they'd gone. They were running without lights.

Loughlin said, "They'll be on the telephone to every airfield and we should see some pursuit soon."

Stone looked upward; the sky was overcast, very

misty. They should be hard to spot. But they were in the open. He pointed upward.

"Get us into the clouds."

Hog eased the chopper above the streaky clouds and they raced along only a few yards above them, their wake churning clouds into smoke.

Listening to the radio, Anna gave them reports. Unsure about their direction, the Russians were scrambling fighters in a wide radius about the air base. A helicopter south of Leningrad had been shot down before it was discovered to be on a routine flight for one of the ministries.

"Trigger-happy bastards," Hog observed.

Stone turned to the man just behind him.

The man this had all been for, about, and because of.

One more M.I.A. brought out of harm's way.

Almost.

"How're you doing, Lee?"

"Shook up but alive," Daniels called back. "Are we going to make it?"

"We'll make it," Stone growled. "We're over the Gulf of Finland right now. That puts us out of the Soviet Union, over international waters."

The chopper's rotor noises from above their heads abruptly seemed to grow louder, accompanied by an ominous grinding.

Hog studied his dials.

"We're losing speed, and altitude. I don't know what, but something is sure as hell gone wrong. Musta taken a round or two back at that air base . . ."

The chopper was dropping. Fast.

# Chapter Twenty-three

Loughlin pulled life preservers from a locker and passed them around. Stone shrugged into one and helped Anna into another. The others hurriedly slipped into theirs.

Hog kept working the controls, trying this, trying that, but the Russian chopper just kept losing altitude and speed.

He asked Anna, "Know any Finnish?"

"A couple of words, that's all." Anna shook her head. "But I can try them with Swedish."

"Then do it."

She flicked switches and turned a dial. A babble of static filled the cockpit, then a Russian voice . . . She glanced at him. "They're madder than ever. We are all enemies of the state."

"Get another station."

She settled on a frequency and spoke into a hand mike in Swedish, saying the same things over and over.

Suddenly a male voice cut in and they talked back and forth for several moments. She looked at Stone. "They have us on radar from a ship."

The grinding noise in the chopper had increased and their airspeed had dropped drastically.

Hog called, "We're going in—! When we hit the water, everybody out fast!"

He cut the engine and the rotor clanked to a halt. He fought the controls.

And in the next second they were in the water.

The sea was cold but calm. For a few minutes the chopper bobbed, rocking to the swells. Hog had set the aircraft down expertly and for the moments it floated, they were able to get out and push away.

Loughlin inflated a small dinghy, crawled in, and pulled Daniels in. Hog clambered in and lifted Anna out of the water as easily as pulling a flower. Stone got aboard and they watched the chopper slide beneath the waves.

They were alone in the fog.

Anna pointed. "That way is Finland."

They were in the inflated dinghy only a short time before a Finnish coast guard boat picked them out of the water. It was a sleek, silver cutter with black numbers painted on the prow. It loomed out of the white mist and a seaman yelled; the engines stopped and the rubber boat bumped the hull.

The skipper, a young lieutenant, spoke passable English. "You escaped from Russia?"

"We didn't get along worth a damn," Hog told him.

The cutter took them to Helsinki. The radio had flashed the word to a waiting world that American journalist, Lee Daniels, had been snatched from the jaws of the K.G.B.

The news dominated the media and a hundred news-people were crowding the docks as the cutter arrived and slid into her berth. The lieutenant and his officers escorted Daniels off the ship where they were instantly engulfed by shouting reporters, welcomers, and government officials. Flashbulbs punctuated the scene and a hundred cameras clicked.

Stone and the others watched from the deck, happy to let Daniels have the glory. When the mob had gone, they slipped off the cutter unobserved.

The State Department had flown Daniels's family to meet him. They arrived next day amid more reporters and cameras.

After a doctor's examination, Daniels was interviewed by reporters and commentators. The story of how he had been detained by the K.G.B. and drugged caused a huge wave of resentment against the Soviet government.

The doctors agreed that Daniels had been drugged and poorly treated. He was more than ten pounds lighter than he had been at the time of his capture. He had not been beaten but had expected it at any time, he told them.

The Soviet authorities denied everything Daniels said. According to *Pravda* the newsman had fabricated the entire story. Where was the helicopter Daniels said he had escaped in? Could he produce it?

The idea that foreigners could come into the Soviet Union and free someone was ridiculous on the face of it. Daniels was obviously suffering some mysterious delusion.

The Colonel Zarnov that Daniels had mentioned had not been in Moscow at the time. He was stationed in

East Germany and was interviewed there, stating he had never heard of Lee Daniels.

Stone, Hog, and Loughlin made a complete report to Senator Harler, with names and dates. They had come to West Germany at the senator's request and were staying at the Bingham House, an American hotel used by politicians and large firms. Their suite was on the fourteenth floor, just above Harler's.

It took several days to dictate the report and transcribe it to their satisfaction.

Anna stayed with them only one day, putting down her part in the affair. Then, with fond good-byes all round, she took a plane for Sweden and home.

When the report was finished, Harler read it through once more, saying the Senate would hear all of it when he returned to Washington. It showed the Soviets in their true light, professing one thing and doing quite another. Many newsmen, in their handling of the Daniels affair, recalled the Korean airliner disaster, reminding their readers of the worth of Soviet statements.

While Senator Harler studied the report, Stone, Hog, and Loughlin remained in their suite at his request. They had gained a certain fame as M.I.A. hunters and he felt it would be better if reporters did not connect them to this Russian adventure . . . at least not for the moment.

They had lost their weapons in the Gulf of Finland and felt naked, they told Harler, without them.

Harler pulled strings to get three .45 Colt pistols delivered to them at the hotel. "But please," he asked, "do not shoot any Germans."

Cleaning kits and spare clips came with the package, as well as shoulder holsters and ammo.

Mark Stone stood before a mirror adjusting the

leather shoulder holster. The .45 automatic, fully loaded, was a heavy piece of artillery. It was also a difficult piece to get used to, but it had an awesome punch and it was very dependable.

In the next room Loughlin was prattling about London, saying he knew a few places where they would be treated like kings. He was suggesting they go there as soon as Harler was finished with them. Hog was all for it.

Stone heard the rap on the door.

Hog called, "Who is it?"

A voice: "Room service, sir."

Loughlin said, "I didn't order anything—did you?"

Then something slammed into the door, it burst open and three men ran in, Uzis chattering.

Hog Wiley and Loughlin hit the floor at the first sound. The .45-calibers pounded lead. The leading intruder crumpled, spurting blood. The man behind him whirled about, the submachine gun slashing holes in the ceiling.

Stone jumped to the doorway and fired at the third man, seeing his head dissolve into a red ruin.

It had been Gregg, the C.I.A. man from Moscow.

A double agent, terminated.

Acrid powder smoke filled the air.

"Everyone okay?" Hog asked.

"What the bloody hell!" Loughlin said.

Stone moved to the hall door. He heard footsteps.

Ducking down, he peered around the jamb. A hail of bullets followed the movement, shattering the wood. He pulled back but he had seen a dark figure running. Was it Zarnov?

He looked around the door again quickly. The figure had reached the back stairway. Jumping into the hall, Stone fired three times. He saw bits of plaster jump off the wall but the figure was gone.

Pushing the button to release the clip, he shoved in a fresh one and ran down the corridor as Hog yelled behind him.

He looked over the rail and a vicious burst from the other's Uzi shredded the wood beside him. He glanced back to see Hog and Loughlin coming. He ran down the steps past the landing and paused at the next floor. Kneeling, he looked around the corner and drew back instantly.

His assailant was standing in the hall a dozen yards away and the Uzi slammed bullets, ripping and tearing the corner.

When he heard footsteps, Stone jumped into the hall and fired four shots and saw the man stumble. The assailant fell against the wall, leaving a red smear, but he did not drop the submachine gun. He reeled against a door and it opened.

A woman screamed.

Stone dashed toward the door.

There were more screams from inside the room and a man's voice shouting something in outrage. Stone looked round the door.

It *was* Zarnov!

The man was limping toward the far wall, looking back over his shoulder. He turned as Stone stepped into the room.

Stone fired twice as Zarnov raised the Uzi. The great punch of the .45 knocked Zarnov into the picture window. Glass shattered and the Russian was hurled out into space several stories above street level.

The K.G.B. boss screamed all the way down.